you're
so
Beautiful

you're so Beautiful

STORIES

BY

EILEEN

FITZGERALD

ST. MARTIN'S GRIFFIN 🐦 NEW YORK

These stories first appeared in the following magazines:

"Sister Boom-Boom" in *Prairie Schooner*; "Zoo Bus" in *The Iowa Review*; "You're So Beautiful" in *Puerto del Sol*; "Thunderation" in *Other Voices*; "Annies" in *Hopewell Review*; "Chicken Train" in *Crab Orchard Review*.

YOU'RE SO BEAUTIFUL. Copyright © 1996 by Eileen FitzGerald. All rights reserved. Printed in the United States of America. No part of this book may be used or reproduced in any manner whatsoever without written permission except in the case of brief quotations embodied in critical articles or reviews. For information, address St. Martin's Press, 175 Fifth Avenue, New York, N.Y. 10010.

Design by Pei Koay

Library of Congress Cataloging-in-Publication Data

FitzGerald, Eileen.
    You're so beautiful: stories / by Eileen FitzGerald.—
1st ed.
        p.   cm.
    ISBN 0-312-17069-6
    I. Title.
    PS3556.I83Y68   1996
    813'.54—dc20   96-20054
                                                                    CIP

First St. Martin's Griffin Edition: September 1997

10   9   8   7   6   5   4   3   2   1

For J.D.

ACKNOWLEDGMENTS

I'm grateful to my family and others who have helped me with my stories: Mary T. Lane, Barbara Bean, Lizanne Minerva, Jesse Lee Kercheval, and Anne Savarese. I'd also like to thank the Wisconsin Institute for Creative Writing for a year of support and good company.

CONTENTS

you're
So
Beautiful

*A*s she sang her number for the talent show, Courtney reached toward the audience with pleading gestures, stretching her fingers so wide that her hands looked like starfish. She swayed and occasionally stepped left or right; the spotlight wobbled trying to keep track of her. Jean, Courtney's mother, played the piano and waited for tears. Earlier in the week, Courtney had mentioned that she might try to cry at the end of "Send in the Clowns."

Jean's younger daughter, Brenda, thought it might be a good idea, but Jean disagreed. "Don't be cheap," she'd said. "Just sing the song. You have a nice voice." Courtney's voice was pleasant and undistinguished, but the stage movements made her seem jaded, like an entertainer who has been reduced to giving free concerts in amusement parks. Jean wondered where she'd learned such melodramatic movements—from the "Midnight Special," the "Jerry Lewis Telethon"? Standing in the wings, waiting for their cue, they'd watched the act before Courtney's. "Crying for a song," Jean whispered, "is about as subtle as going braless in the rain." Courtney nodded noncommittally.

Courtney wore last year's prom dress, a slinky, sky blue evening gown. The spaghetti straps, so provocative a year ago, now looked limp and pathetic, and Jean was sorry she'd suggested it. Perhaps a prom dress was a one-occasion dress, like a wedding dress or a bridesmaid's dress; Jean's theory was that the big event—the joy and perspiration—dissolved the dress's shimmer. Perhaps it was a garment industry conspiracy. What Jean knew for sure was that a wedding dress away from its wedding became lumpy and ill fitting. For her own wedding, Jean, twenty-five and practical, had selected a white suit. Afterward, she had it dyed navy blue. In the early days of marriage, she wore it a few times for grocery shopping, but she always felt awkward and overdressed; the suit was too fancy for errands, too stern for parties. If she'd had a job, she could have worn it to the office, but she didn't work then. Darrell hadn't wanted her to.

Jean focused on the page of notes before her, on the slick feel of the piano keys beneath her fingers. Her body felt hulking and strange perched on the piano bench in the high school auditorium. One leg of her pantyhose was twisted. When she pressed the pedals on the piano, the nylon clutched her thigh like a girdle.

Somewhere in the darkened auditorium, Jean's ex-husband, Darrell, sat with his new wife, Crystal. Darrell and Crystal and Jean, breathing the same air, all of them, inhaling and exhaling the same little molecules. Jean squashed the thought and turned the page. The divorce had been almost five years before, and she tried not to think about Darrell.

Ordinarily Courtney would have gotten Friday night tickets for Jean, Saturday night tickets for Darrell and Crystal, and they all would have continued peacefully in their separate lives. Ordinarily Jean would not be onstage at the high school talent show, but Courtney hadn't been able to find an accompanist. Jean enjoyed being with Courtney and Brenda, but she didn't want her daughters to think she was always tagging along, like a pesky sister. She hesitantly offered to help, and Courtney accepted. Jean had fun at the practices, chatting with the performers and the backstage crew. She was the only parent in the talent show, but she didn't let that bother her. She'd done sillier things in her life, monumentally silly things. She'd been a nun, for instance; she'd married Darrell. Playing the piano at the high school talent show was no more ridiculous than the great pride she used to feel when she made a nice meatloaf. As she got older, she cared less about what other people—especially people she hardly knew—thought about her. Dandelions grew wild in her yard, and paint fell off her house in clumps and curls; the neighborhood association sent notes and reprimands. There were rules about lawns reverting to meadows, rules against houses falling into disrepair. Jean did her best, but didn't worry.

She had memorized the song, but she concentrated on the notes anyway. There was nowhere else to look. If she looked at Courtney, she would see the sad prom dress and maybe fake tears. If she looked into the audience, she might see Darrell and Crystal scrutinizing her; she might lose her place, forget the tune. If the places were reversed, if Darrell was playing the piano and Jean was in the audience, she would stare at him through binoculars, jot down his wrinkles and his hairline. He was the man she was supposed to grow old with; she felt obliged to take note. On the occasions when she spoke with him about money or problems with the girls, she was too preoccupied with appearing nonchalant to pay close attention to his appearance.

Courtney made it through "Goodbye, Yellow Brick Road" with dry eyes. One more song, and then it was over. Jean dreaded the post-show milling and gathering as families and friends met in the foyer to congratulate the performers. Last night she'd talked with Courtney and Brenda and their friends, and they'd all had an amiable time. Tonight, though, it would be Jean and Courtney and Darrell and Crystal standing together, staring at one another. Jean would extend her hand to Crystal and say, "How do you do?" She would be gracious, poised, controlled. She would not, however, say, "Glad to meet you."

She would not cry, either. The years for crying over Darrell were long past. Darrell and Crystal had a life together now, five years of marriage, and two small girls: Melanie and Meredith. Crystal's Christmas fruitcakes and Thanksgiving turkeys were gradually blotting out Jean's. Darrell and Jean's fifteen-year marriage—even the memory of it—was fading away. Fair enough. Jean was doing her own part to blot out the past. She'd established her own holiday traditions—caroling with the church choir, helping serve food at a homeless shelter.

Because they lived less than twelve city blocks apart, Jean and Crystal occasionally overlapped at Milgrim's. Usually she just caught a distant glimpse, but to Jean it seemed mathematically likely that they would meet head-on someday, somewhere, maybe by the cereal, maybe by the pickles, maybe under the big sign that said Hi, Neighbor! The first time she saw Crystal in the store had been almost a year after Darrell left. A year wasn't much time, but it was enough. Still, Jean had wanted to yank out bunches of Crystal's hair. She wanted to yell, "This is *my* store!" She had wanted to notify the manager, tell him that she'd been a customer for twenty years, that it wasn't *fair*. This was when Crystal was impossibly young, before she had babies, before she came to seem more disheveled and more human. Jean stood behind her in the checkout line, holding tight to the handle of her shopping cart, fortifying herself with steady breathing—if Crystal looked back, Jean would say hello. But Crystal lifted her groceries onto the conveyor belt without a glance, without a blink. Jean itched to know if Crystal was ignoring her or if she truly hadn't noticed. Surely Crystal knew who she was; surely she'd seen a picture. Hadn't Darrell ever pointed out the car window and said, "That's her"? Hadn't Crystal ever driven by and seen Jean working in the yard, pushing the lawn mower or hacking at the bushes?

Crystal's groceries sprawled along the conveyor belt: lettuce, yogurt, Alpha-bits cereal, plastic-wrapped pork chops, a tomato. Jean thought of tapping Crystal on the shoulder. She opened her mouth to speak. She would say, "Hi, there." If she didn't say hello now, it would

4

only get more difficult. Once a week, for the next fifty years, Jean would stand behind Crystal, sweating and afraid. She closed her mouth, opened it, closed it. Her saliva tasted like pennies. Crystal faced the big front windows and waited for the bag boy to check the price of her lettuce. "Eighty-eight cents per pound?" said Crystal. "I thought it was eighty-eight cents per lettuce." The line behind Jean extended into the frozen foods, past the waffles, past the pizzas.

Peeking at Crystal, Jean ran her fingers along the rubber conveyor belt. She slid one finger across until it touched Crystal's tomato. She wasn't sure why she wanted to touch the tomato; she just did.

The cashier in the next aisle moved a steady stream of groceries into the wide mouths of brown bags. She processed three customers while Crystal and Jean and the other people in line waited for Crystal's lettuce.

Jean meant only to touch the tomato, but with her finger brushing the silken skin, she felt a flash of anger, at Darrell, at Crystal, at both of them, at everything. She would never be such a perfect thing, so shining in the sun. She'd never be twenty-one, with mascara and blue eyeshadow. Jean's thumb curled around, her hand surrounded the tomato, and she gave it a bruising pinch. Crystal stared out the window, oblivious. Swinging the bag of lettuce lasso style, the boy returned; the cashier punched in the numbers, the dented tomato traveled slowly forward on the black rubber belt.

Afterward, Jean regretted what she had done. She thought of leaving an anonymous tomato on Darrell and Crystal's doorstep, but the chance of being caught and humiliated was too great. She pictured herself handing over the tomato, Darrell absolving her from sin. A new tomato would be inadequate penance anyway. It could be diced for a salad, sliced for sandwiches, but it couldn't negate Jean's surge of ill will. She couldn't erase the fact of her feelings with a tomato.

Since that time Jean often spotted Crystal in stores and in the neighborhood. Early on, she saw Crystal jogging along Ward Parkway in bright-colored shorts and T-shirts. Then she saw her walking in the park, slowed by pregnancy. Seeing Crystal's maternity dress, her pink, round face, Jean thought of being pregnant herself. She thought of how Darrell would sing songs and whisper silly names into her belly button: Sparky, Skippy, Champ. Together they had marveled at the changes in Jean's body. *"This* is the miracle," they said. "This is the only miracle there is." Before Darrell left, Jean had wanted another baby, but that day, when she saw Crystal's full belly, Jean knew her time was out; she knew she never would.

Later, Jean saw Crystal pushing a stroller that held one baby and then two. They never spoke. Once Jean had moved past the ugliest part of her sadness, she was willing enough to nod, to smile, to help Crystal lift the stroller over rough pavement, but Crystal never looked her way. But now, with Courtney due to graduate next year, Crystal and Jean and Darrell were inching inevitably closer to being in the same room, to being in a conversation. It could happen tonight.

The idea was unnerving, but the actual meeting might not be so bad. Talking with Crystal might even be interesting; Jean could ask if Darrell still got nauseous at the thought of changing a diaper. Once, when Darrell was baby-sitting alone, he had driven to Jean's mother's house so she could change Courtney. Jean could tell Crystal about that. It wasn't the sort of story that Darrell would tell on himself.

Courtney was smiling at the end of her song. She bowed and did a sort of curtsey. Jean wanted to hug her, but instead she stood stiff by the piano, letting Courtney soak in her applause. In the wings, Jean kissed her cheek. "You're wonderful," she whispered, then slipped past the students who huddled backstage, tucked in among the curtain folds. She made her way through the spooky underbelly of the school, through the locker rooms and silent corridors and up another set of stairs to the balcony, where she settled herself on a bleacher to watch the chunky modern dancer, the strange, skinny ventriloquist.

Jean admired all the performers. It took courage to stand on a big stage and sing or dance or play the flute. But when the rock band began to play, she headed down to the cafeteria. She liked the boys and their self-conscious, synchronized dance moves, but they played too loud for her enjoyment. At the refreshment table, she bought a Coke in a limp paper cup. She took a careful sip. She could skip the mingling, she thought. She had mingled the night before. She could wait in the car until Courtney was ready. But really, she assured herself, there was no reason to worry. She could talk with Darrell easily enough; she talked to him when she had to. And Crystal—she wasn't worried about Crystal. She and Crystal would get along fine.

The band played on. Jean drank her Coke. She watched one parent after another open the auditorium door just enough to squeeze through, then close it gently against the noise. In the foyer they blinked and poked at their ears, adjusting to the bright light, the relative quiet. Jean wondered if they felt as old as she did, older than she'd ever intended to be. She walked into the bathroom, threw the cup into the trash can, took her hairbrush from her purse. She looked—not bad. The dash of green eye shadow that Courtney had applied brought out the color of her dress and coaxed the green flecks in her eyes to the surface. She thought she might wear a little to work next week, see if it gave some zing to her typing. Her hair was short and curly and thick, a sporty cut. She'd had long hair like Crystal's—pretty hair— when she married Darrell, but with small children the upkeep became too bothersome. She wondered if Crystal would keep her hair long now that she had two babies to care for. Maybe long hair meant more to Crystal than it had to Jean. Maybe it meant more to Darrell than Jean had realized.

At eighteen, just before she took her religious vows, Jean had cut her hair short and ugly, for love of God. By twenty-four, though, she was no longer sure she had a calling. Playing the guitar at mass gave her pleasure, but little else did, not meals with the other sisters, not prayers, not her administrative work at the parish grade school. It was a time when many religious left their orders; Darrell quit the priesthood then. Some people left because the Church was changing too quickly, some because it was changing too slowly. Jean left because of changes in herself, because her prayers had become as meaningless and heavy as rocks. At twenty-five, she was a lay person again, and she vowed to let her hair grow long; she vowed to be beautiful. After she married Darrell, she frosted her hair, bought a few miniskirts. He called her Sister Boom-Boom.

The bathroom door creaked open. Jean pulled the brush through her hair again, then saw another face beside hers in the mirror. She saw eyes, brown eyes, and those eyes saw her, and then Jean realized who she was looking at.

Startled, Jean held the hairbrush in front of her, as if she were offering it to the image in the mirror. "Oh," she said. "Crystal."

Crystal averted her eyes. She pumped some soap grains out of the dispenser. She turned on the water and rubbed her hands under the stream. She kept her head down and said nothing. She shook her hands dry and left the bathroom.

Jean stood stupidly, watching the arc of the door as it eased closed. Maybe Crystal knew about the tomato and hated Jean because of it. If so, it was an extreme reaction, Jean thought, considering the hurt that Crystal had caused. She wondered what would happen if she went into the foyer and sought out Darrell and Crystal, and stood near them, stood behind them. Would Crystal say hello then? Or would they both ignore her?

When Jean finally walked out, she saw Courtney and Darrell and Crystal standing in a tight circle halfway across the crowded foyer. She watched the threesome. In a move so perfectly timed that it seemed choreographed, Darrell embraced Courtney, then Crystal did, and as Jean took the first step toward them, Darrell and Crystal walked past the plaques listing fifty years of wrestling champions, to the red double doors, and were gone.

Seven or eight months after the divorce was final, Darrell had shown up unannounced. Jean invited him in—how strange it had been to invite him into the house he'd lived in for years, the house he'd painted and repaired. She gave him apple juice in a heavy tumbler made of nubbled glass, part of a set his brother had given them one Christmas long before. He rubbed his fingers over the bumps, turned the glass in his hand. He held it familiarly, but studied it carefully, as if it were an ancient artifact.

Perhaps, Jean thought, he just wanted to talk.

"I always liked these glasses," said Darrell.

"Sure," said Jean. "Me, too." She told him about the girls, about school, funny stories, problems. Sometimes, in lonely daydreams, she thought about what she'd do if he asked to come back. She laughed over the absurdity of hoping, then wondered, would she let him back? "No," was what she told the dream Darrell. "I have my own life now." It would be too difficult to fit him back in. The laundry and cooking schedules had gotten relaxed, and Darrell valued order. For years she'd struggled to keep up with his sweaty running clothes; she wouldn't do that again. She knew people who ended up together after long separations, after divorce, even. From the vantage point of secure marriages, they referred to those past years as rough spots. But Jean knew this was more than a bump in the road; it was an enormous pothole, a bridge out.

Darrell drained his glass, working to get every drop of liquid. Jean thought of how he ate apples down to the core, and then gave pious little lectures about waste not, want not. He leaned forward in his chair, more formal than friendly. "I was wondering," he said, in words that seemed rehearsed, "if I could have the wedding pictures. They can only be unhappy memories for you now, after what's happened."

Jean stared, unable to speak.

"You got the house and the furniture," said Darrell. "I'd like the pictures. It's a small thing."

The living room was shabby, but felt familiar and homey to Jean. A person could get used to anything, water stains on the walls, floors that slanted—with time a person could get used to no roof or a six-foot pit in the middle of the floor. When Darrell left, they'd been in the midst of removing the layers and layers of old wallpaper. In the first days of loneliness, she'd been in a panic over how to finish the walls herself. Finally, she returned the rented steamer and painted over the lumps. She wondered if Darrell remembered the paper curling off the walls, the hot, moist air, the whole unfinished project.

"I also got two children who like to sit in chairs and sleep in beds," she said. "If you'll remember, there was a reason why I got the house and furniture. Don't you understand that we're only scraping by? Didn't I just tell you Brenda needs a crown on her tooth?"

"Relax, okay, just relax." Darrell leaned back in the plaid armchair, easily, comfortably. It was a chair he knew well. "I think of you sitting here, all alone, turning the pages, it depresses me."

"If I looked at the pictures—which I don't—it would be so I could laugh at your funny haircut and your big ears. I wouldn't be depressed at all." She was embarrassed to be taking such silly swipes, but she couldn't think of how to fight reasonably. She couldn't think with him sitting in the house, drinking apple juice.

"Why won't you just give them to me?"

"Tell me why you want them." He knew where the album was; he could take them and march out. She didn't think he would do that, but she never thought he would leave her for a twenty-year-old either.

Finally he told her: Crystal wanted the pictures.

She realized then why he'd come, not to talk, not to rescue her. He'd come to erase her.

"Listen to me, Jean." Darrell spoke to her slowly, as if she was a crazy person. She waited for him to grab her beneath the chin, to force her to look into his eyes. "This part of my life—our life—is dead and over, and I want to be certain you're not mooning over the pictures, living in the past. You can trust that I'll do what's best."

"That's what it's all about, isn't it? Trust."

He flicked the glass once sharply with his fingernail. "Funny."

"I'm funny. You're a Boy Scout. That's all fine and good. But you may *not* have the wedding pictures, ever. If you like I'll cut your little head out of all the pictures and you can take those home with you." She tried to understand how this had happened, how Darrell had ended up in her living room, asking for the wedding pictures. Crystal had made him, but why did she care?

"I knew you would get hysterical." He was talking more to himself than to Jean. "But I thought, she's surprised me before; when I thought she'd get crazy, she's stayed calm. I'm trying to help. I don't want you to live in the past."

"You don't want there to be a past. But there is a past and there's a Courtney and a Brenda and me, and we're the past, Darrell, and we aren't going away. Crystal can pretend that she's your first and only love, she can pretend that you're high school sweethearts, she can pretend all she wants, but she's going to have to get used to me being around."

And on it went. Perhaps it was the fight they should have had when he came to fill his suitcases with socks and underwear to take to Crystal's apartment. Then Jean was so stunned, so passive, she actually knelt beside her bed and prayed. She needed a steady mumble of words to fill the dead spaces in her brain. She wasn't asking for a miracle; she wasn't talking to a god. She was telling herself the story of her life, over and over.

In the end she gave him one picture. She hadn't taken the album from its box in years. When she opened it, the pictures were familiar but distant, quaint and naive; she didn't want to look.

As soon as she loosened the photo from the stiff page, she knew she was making a mistake to give him even this much. Handing it over, she felt like she was inside an old movie where a pile of yellowed letters swirl in the wind and then blow away. Over time the album began to disassemble itself. Brenda used a picture in an art project, a collage of her life. Later, Jean took out a photograph of herself that she'd always liked and put it on her dresser. She hadn't looked at the album since then; she didn't know what further erosion had taken place.

All around her, people were talking in groups, with one or two giggling, flushed-faced performers at the center of attention. Courtney had been swallowed up by a group of girls. Jean walked over slowly and stood behind her. She wouldn't mind joining the conversation if someone gave her a way in. But no one noticed her; no one pulled her in with a question or a wink. Such cocktail party skills came after high school. Finally Jean tapped Courtney on the shoulder.

"Need a ride?" Jean asked.

Courtney surveyed her group of friends, the crowded cafeteria. "I'll get one," she said.

At home that night, sitting in warm bathwater, Jean shaved her legs and pondered Crystal. Maybe she was shy, Jean reasoned, maybe Crystal had wanted to say hello in the high school restroom, but she'd been petrified with fear. She'd washed her hands, hoping for courage, then she fled. It was easier for her to pretend that Jean didn't exist.

If the chasm between them was ever going to close, Jean knew she would have to make the overture. They couldn't meet in the middle; Jean was going to have to walk all the way over to Crystal's side. She could do that. But she'd need a way to explain herself when she got there. Lying in bed, she came up with a solution, a segue, a footbridge.

In the morning, the plan still seemed sound. Jean ate a bowl of Special K and poked at the idea, testing for weak spots. She wondered how much it would hurt. Probably it would feel like a big bruise, like the ache of too many sit-ups. From the stairwell came the plump and swish of clothes flying through the air. Brenda kicked and cursed at the laundry pile. Courtney sat at the table in a brown waitress uniform, drinking Dr. Pepper and eating slices of deli roast beef. Her hair was wet from the shower, but her face still showed bits of orange stage makeup among patches of acne.

"I'm thinking of having my tubes tied," said Jean.

"Interesting." Courtney tipped another inch of soda into her glass. "Can I get a nose job?"

"Of course not. You're perfect the way you are."

"Why doesn't someone in this pigpen wash some clothes?!" shouted Brenda.

"Why don't *you?*" said Courtney, not quite loud enough for Brenda to hear.

"I was thinking I would call Crystal and see if she would drive me." Courtney screwed the top back on the bottle. She looked at Jean.

There were other possibilities, of course. She could call Crystal and suggest that they go together to donate blood. Once, she and a neighbor gave blood together and then had a giddy, giggly time eating the cookies afterward. They could go shopping or see a movie. All were possibilities, but the tubes were foolproof. On her driver's license, Jean had marked the place for organ donor so that when she died someone else would get a new life from her kidneys and other organs. To exchange her fallopian tubes for friendship was not much different. On the drive to the hospital, she could pretend that it was necessary surgery and gain Crystal's sympathy. Or she could admit it was voluntary, and they could talk about sex.

Jean's actual sex life was unremarkable. She'd met a man named Max at a church singles' group, and whenever he asked her to go out, she would. They'd spent three nights together over the past few months, but she didn't think she'd sleep with him anymore. She didn't like him enough to be naked with him again.

Brenda ranted from the stairwell. "That's it. I'm calling in sick. Courtney, you tell them I can't fucking find my fucking uniform." She stuck her head into the kitchen, then screamed. She ran to the table in her bra and panties and grabbed at the collar of Courtney's uniform. "Mine!" she shouted. "The size twelve is mine! Take it off—Mom, make her take it off."

"God, ouch! Get away." Courtney held off Brenda's arms.

"Girls," said Jean. She reached into the laundry room and pulled out a brown uniform on a wire hanger. "There's plenty for everyone."

"You're the best mommy." Brenda hugged her, instantly placated. "Did you wash that for me? If it's a size eight, I can't wear it. It won't button." Brenda checked the tag. "Okay, ten." She dressed in the middle of the kitchen. "Ooof," she said, tugging at the buttons.

"Mom is getting her tubes tied," said Courtney.

"Who do you have sex with?" Reaching up under her dress, Brenda pulled off her panties and threw them toward the laundry pile, missing by several feet. Jean took a clean pair from the laundry basket under the table and handed them to Brenda.

"Who do you think?"

"Max?!" screamed Brenda. "Gross."

"Yikes," said Courtney.

"Stranger things have happened," said Jean. "It started to seem a little useless to save myself for Mel Gibson."

"Tell her the other part," said Courtney.

"I'm going to ask Crystal if she'll drive me."

"What?" Brenda opened her eyes wide and looked at Courtney. "Why?"

"Why doesn't Max drive you?" asked Courtney.

"It's an outpatient procedure—I think it is—so it would be a nice chance for us to get to know each other, driving over and sitting in the waiting room. Crystal is a part of your lives, and I feel that I should get to know her."

"Sure," said Brenda. "Get to know her. Invite her over for tea. Don't have her drive you around. Don't be weird."

"A tea party," said Courtney. "I'll make lemon bars."

"Great." Brenda nodded. "And I'll make those cookies with all the stuff in them, those chocolate chip layer cookies, the coconut ones. Crystal likes those."

Outside a horn honked, Brenda and Courtney's ride to the restaurant. "Don't call her till we get back," said Brenda. "Don't do anything." They ran out of the house, grabbing aprons, purses, roast beef.

So Crystal liked layer cookies. This was the first Jean had heard of it. She'd made those cookies before. She tried to remember the ingredients: coconut, chocolate chips, walnuts, graham crackers on the bottom—did butter count as a layer?—something else . . . Jean reached for the cookbook, then remembered: condensed milk. Gummy, grayish sweetened condensed milk. There had been a time when Jean kept the house steadily supplied with homemade cookies. She could make some for the drive to the hospital. Probably Jean wouldn't be able to eat any before surgery, but she could bring them for Crystal to enjoy.

Crystal would never come over for an awkward afternoon of tea, not even if there were cookie bars. Jean didn't know Crystal, but she knew that. If Jean needed help, though, Crystal might pitch in; they might end up being friends.

Courtney had written the number in the phone book under *Dad*. Jean wondered if she should get a doctor's appointment first, then call Crystal, or if she should present it as an abstract idea first, and see how Crystal reacted. Don't call, the girls had said, but she had the momentum; she dialed without rehearsing what she would say.

She waited through three rings, then Darrell answered, a second later Crystal picked up the phone and said hello.

"Crystal?" said Jean.

"Got it, honey?" Darrell hung up his phone.

"Yes?" said Crystal.

"Hi, Crystal. This is Jean."

Jean heard an intake of breath, then silence. She heard a click, then a dial tone. . . .

Maybe it was a leftover from the time before Darrell and Crystal got their apartment together, from the early days of covert romance. Perhaps Crystal had gotten in the habit of quickly hanging up the phone when she heard Jean's voice. Or maybe she was deathly shy, not just face-to-face in the mirror shy—anyone would be shy under those circumstances—but maybe she was telephone shy, too. Maybe Crystal was holding the phone now, cursing her foolishness. Jean gave her another chance.

"She's not available," said Darrell.

"Maybe when she's available, she could give me a call."

"I'll leave the message," said Darrell. "How'd it feel being up there playing the piano last night?"

"I enjoyed it." Jean said good-bye. She walked over to Brenda's panties, threw them onto the dirty clothes heap. The phone rang.

Part of her wanted to let it ring and ring. Part of her was too tired to answer. But she moved to the phone, reached out her hand.

"Mom," said Brenda. "I just wanted to say that I think that doing the tube thing is pretty extreme. But it's your life, right, it's your body, and if you really want to, I'll drive you."

"Baby, you can't drive me. A young girl cannot drive her mother to get her tubes tied."

"It's not like I'm dying to do it, but I will."

"It confuses the natural order of things. It can't be. Anyway," she said, "it's just an idea. I'm not going to rush into anything."

"Okay, well, don't call Crystal. We'll be back soon. It's pretty slow, and they're sending people home. I love you."

Then she heard Courtney's voice in the distance. "I love you, Mommy."

Jean hung up the phone and began tidying the kitchen. Courtney had left a container of lip gloss on the table; Jean uncapped the small glass bottle, breathed in the exuberant strawberry smell. Over the years, on weekend visits, Crystal had taught the girls how to do makeup, a skill that Jean had never mastered. When Jean was in high school, it didn't even occur to her to wear lipstick. That was something other girls did. Instead, she started a Devotion to Mary club that met at lunchtime to say the rosary. She spent her time doing good deeds, trying to be a saint. After the weekend visits with Darrell and Crystal, the girls came home with beauty pageant faces and shopping lists. "Crystal says we need good brushes, all different sizes. Crystal says—"

The summer before Courtney started high school, Jean wrote separate notes to Brenda and Courtney and left them on their pillows:

> *Sex is a beautiful thing. Children are wonderful, but pregnancy could change your life. Don't take stupid chances. If you are thinking about having sex, let me know so that we can set up a GYN appt. (If you are already having sex, let me know and we will go right away!!) I love you,*
>
> *Mommy*

Jean wiped the table with a wet sponge, brushing the crumbs into her hand. Maybe Crystal was the one to teach the girls how to apply blush, but Jean was the one to teach them about sex, about love. She was the one to take the girls to their first gynecological appointments. Still, alone on weekends, Jean wondered what Crystal and Courtney and Brenda did together. She wondered how deep Crystal's influence was.

Of course, the practical solution was to get a diaphragm and wait for the change of life. She'd probably never see Max again, much less sleep with him. Why worry about Crystal? If they had to chat at graduation, so be it. If they had to stand together in a receiving line at Courtney or Brenda's wedding, they'd manage somehow.

The next morning the girls showed Jean the list they'd made at work: food, flowers, napkins, teacups, milk, Dr. Pepper. "I changed my mind," said Jean, but they were set on the idea of a tea party.

"Do you want Dad to come?" asked Brenda.

"She wants to be friends with Crystal," said Courtney. "Dad already had his chance."

Brenda wrote notes on a tablet. "You have to know how to deal with Crystal. You have to sort of trick her into doing things. That's what Dad does. You make her think something is her idea and then she'll do it."

For a week, they plotted and strategized, but when they finally called, Crystal declined.

"It's plain rude," said Brenda.

"She's too busy. So she says." Courtney ripped the party notes into tiny pieces.

"Did you tell her I ironed the tablecloth?" asked Brenda. "Did you tell her that?"

"It's her choice," said Jean. "If she doesn't want to, she doesn't want to."

They decided to have the tea party anyway; they would wear hats and gloves and dresses, invite friends. They'd use the pressed tablecloth and play classical music.

On Friday, Jean drove to Milgrim's for supplies: tea, toilet paper, coconut. Winding through the store, she thought of the straw hat she'd bought at Kmart, floppy with a big, red bow. She'd wear a flowery, summery dress, though it was nearing November and quite chilly on some days. They'd have fun despite Crystal. Jean turned her cart into the baking aisle—and stopped short. Crystal.

In that first moment, Jean could have slipped away unseen, but she'd come for coconut, and this was where she'd find it. She directed her cart toward Crystal, who stood in front of the Pop-Tart display.

Smiling, Jean made one last attempt. "I like the cinnamon."

Crystal said nothing. Her lips pursed and her face iced over. Jean swallowed a sigh, dipped down to grab the bag of coconut. When she straightened, she saw that Crystal was moving away. Jean stared for a moment at the neatly stacked boxes, the seemingly endless variety of toaster pastries. Then, pushing her shopping cart onward, Jean thought back. She thought of the pie.

A month or so after Darrell left, once he'd settled into an apartment with Crystal, he asked the girls to spend a weekend with him. Jean sent a pie. When she thought about it now, she couldn't remember the reason for making it. She hadn't often made pies—her family preferred chocolate cake—and she hadn't made a pie since, though there were parts of the making that she had enjoyed: flattening the dough with her mother's heavy rolling pin, scalloping the edges of the crust. After the pie was settled in the oven, Jean had sprinkled the extra scraps of crust with cinnamon and sugar and baked them, too; she ate them herself that night. She soaked in the tub and read from Courtney's stack of *People* magazines until her brain got mushy with celebrity news. She wondered how Darrell and the girls were entertaining themselves. Would they play a board game, talk, watch a TV movie? She wondered what Crystal was like—she'd never met a Crystal before; it sounded like a name for a prostitute, or a parakeet. Reading and bathing and lying on her bed, waiting and waiting, the whole time she tried to imagine what they were doing. She wondered who would cut the pie. Would Darrell? Would Crystal? Would they heat it up? Would they like it?

She found out when the girls returned.

"We sat on the floor," said Brenda, "and we ate with forks."

"You didn't cut pieces and eat on plates?"

"We sat on the floor. There wasn't a table."

"Crystal called it a 'pig-out,' " said Courtney.

Brenda smiled. "It was funny—everyone tried to get as much as they could."

Jean pictured this: Darrell, Courtney, Brenda, and Crystal—all sitting cross-legged on a dusty hardwood floor, wearing dirty-bottomed socks, eating great bites of pie, forks clattering and colliding with other forks and with the pie pan. Steam rose from the battered pastry as from an animal carcass, like a still-warm side of beef in a butcher shop. They ate like dogs tearing into the side of a dead deer. Meanwhile, Jean had leafed through magazines, had nibbled pie crust and relaxed in a bath, content with the life that was left to her.

"Why bother with forks?" Jean asked. "Why didn't you just take turns sticking your faces into the pie?"

"They can do what they want in their own house," Courtney had defended. "No one asked you to make a pie."

When she thought of it later, she could say the words, "It was just a pie," and believe them, almost. But the picture she had imagined stayed sharp—steam rising from the floor, forks clashing noisily.

Rounding the corner into the paper-goods aisle, Jean saw Crystal coming toward her. We'll pass, thought Jean. It's nothing. We'll pass. But as they got closer, Jean saw two boxes of Pop-Tarts in Crystal's basket—chocolate frosted. She thought of Crystal sitting on the floor shoveling in forkfuls of cherry pie, devouring great chunks of Jean's life.

Jean lowered her head. She aimed her cart and pushed mightily, watching the blur of floor tiles, the blur of metal, watching her cart crash into Crystal's. Crystal fell backward onto the floor. She sat stunned, with strands of her long hair tangled in the cart.

"Bitch," said Crystal.

"I'm trying to be nice to you," said Jean.

"You're crazy."

The store manager stood at the end of the aisle wearing a white apron and looking like a fretful baker. Jean handed him money, then rolled by and out the door, taking the coconut with her.

She was on her way to make the cookie bars that Crystal loved. But she wouldn't invite her over; she wouldn't bring her a neighborly plate wrapped with foil. The cookies were not for Crystal.

In the car, Jean laid the bag of coconut beside her in the passenger seat. The plastic package was sticky. When Jean licked her fingers, they tasted sweet.

She was finished with feeling anxious and unsettled, finished with walking the earth like an unburied dead person, finished with waiting for Crystal to give her blessing. In ten years or maybe twenty they could be friends. Maybe. Crystal didn't matter. Crystal could do as she pleased. Jean patted the pillow of coconut. She fastened her seat belt. She blessed herself.

*E*lise opened the blinds and peered through the dusty slats, sifting the traffic for buses. Her feet ached; bones crowded against other bones, almost as if she'd grown extras during her eighty-one years. She leaned against the windowsill. On the street below, a young sweet gum tree held out a scant offering of pointy yellow leaves.

It was just like Gertrude to be late. Elise thought of poking her head out the window, shouting, "Gerrrtruuuude!!" She imagined her sixty-year-old daughter hurrying down the street, trailing a jump rope. Elise almost laughed at the idea of Gertrude coming when she was called, or doing anything she was asked to do.

On the sofa, Alex, her downstairs neighbor, was chewing his ice cubes, although Elise had asked him not to. She shook a finger at him. "Don't eat that glass, Alex. It's part of a set." From now on she would give him hot drinks, nothing he could nibble. Alex was twenty, the age her husband, Bill, had been on their wedding day. Elise tried to remember what it was like to be so young, to believe that one's teeth were immortal. She looked at Alex's long legs, sprawled halfway across her living room. Bill had not been such a casual man; he was a man who sat up straight. He had not been immortal, either. Less than two years after they married, he was killed in a train yard accident. Elise wondered sometimes how her life might have been, if it could have been easier.

In the distance Elise saw the hulking form of a bus. She watched its slow, smoky approach, frowning when she realized that it was the zoo bus. The zebra-striped zoo bus was one of the few old buses that remained in the fleet; the gaudy paint job advertised the African veldt section of the zoo. When Elise had still been riding the city buses—before she broke her collarbone in the bus accident—she made it a point of honor to wait for the next bus, no matter the delay. No self-respecting person rode the zoo bus. Now it groaned to a stop, and Elise watched to see who or what would disembark.

Alex gave his ice another crunch. Usually when he visited, Elise asked him to help with some small task and then rewarded him with a twenty-dollar bill. She decided to make him wait for his money today. She would let him wonder whether he should ask.

"Are you expecting someone?" asked Daniel, Alex's new roommate. His voice startled Elise; she looked to see if she'd mistaken the straight lines of his black hair. She'd always assumed Orientals were boat people, unable to speak English. But Daniel's voice was like a newscaster's, pure American. Elise wondered what he was—Chinese or Japanese? Korean? She knew that Orientals greatly respected their elders. She pictured herself as an Oriental grandmother in a soft, red chair. "Tie my shoe," she would say, and grandchildren would flock to her, anxious to help.

Below, the bus was already moving away, leaving behind a dirty cloud. A woman, grayish brown hair twisted into a tight ballerina bun, stood on the grass patch that separated street and sidewalk, waiting to cross Brookside. Elise turned sharply from the window. "Of course she doesn't look up. Not Gertrude."

"Who's Gertrude?" asked Daniel.

"The daughter," said Alex.

"That's right. My dutiful daughter."

"Listen to this, Daniel—when Gertrude was a baby, she slept in a dresser drawer." Alex laughed. "When it cries you close the drawer."

"It certainly wasn't like that," Elise said stiffly. She turned to Daniel. "It wasn't unheard of," she explained, "to use a box or a basket for a cradle. It was the Depression. A baby doesn't remember."

"Is she coming up?" Daniel looked at Alex. "Should we go?"

Elise laughed. "We would grow cobwebs waiting for Gertrude." She thought of the last time Gertrude had been in this apartment, the day of the last collarbone appointment, the same day the settlement money for the bus accident had arrived. At the doctor's office, Elise had shown the check to the nurse, cupping her hand over the numbers, so Gertrude couldn't see. "I don't want her to slip arsenic into my soup," she whispered.

"Don't be silly," said the nurse. "Your daughter loves you."

After the doctor's appointment, Gertrude and Elise walked to the door, not speaking. Inside the apartment Gertrude made Elise demonstrate her range of motion. "Can you close the shower curtain?" she asked. "Can you function on your own?"

"Of course."

Gertrude stood like a stick figure, feet planted, hands on her hips. "Do you think it's cute? Talking about arsenic?"

"That was a joke," said Elise. "Levity."

"Do you honestly think that's why I'm here? For your money?"

Elise said nothing, and Gertrude left her alone then, with a vaguely aching shoulder and a single thought: The proof is in the pudding.

"Gertrude is a ne'er-do-well," Elise declared. She shook her head, dismissing the topic. But it bothered her, the way Gertrude marched across the street without lifting her hand to wave.

"We'll have lunch," she decided. "Would you boys like lunch?" She knew Alex would go, but she wasn't so sure about Daniel. Maybe he only ate rice.

"I can't," said Alex. "Homework."

Elise turned then to Daniel. "You won't make an old lady eat alone, will you?"

"Certainly not. Lunch sounds great."

Alex lingered by the door until Elise ushered him out. "You study hard," she said, holding his elbow, giving him a tiny push. Her pocketbook hung on the hook by the door; the twenty dollars she'd earmarked for Alex rested inside. She would use the money to buy Daniel's lunch. "We'll go to André's," she said. "Gertrude will probably be there, but we'll just ignore her." There was only so much Elise could do; she couldn't force Gertrude to look up at the window and wave. But she could sit by her at the restaurant. She could sit so close that Gertrude would hear her breathing and know she was alive.

𝒯he door from the street opened into André's sweet shop, where display cases of cakes and chocolates lined the walls. Crocks of jam in wonderful flavors—*fraise, framboise, cassis, citron*—and loaves of shiny, braided bread crowded the shelves and countertops. Elise tilted her head back and inhaled, tasting the rich air with her nose, gripping Daniel's elbow for balance.

Behind the counter, two chocolate dippers were unloading trays of candies. Elise had spoken to the plumper man before; now she waved at him and smiled. "Did you fall in?" she asked, pointing to the chocolate smeared across his white apron.

"Franz dipped me," he said. "I'm selling for ten dollars a pound—going fast."

Elise didn't generally approve of fat people, but she forgave the chocolatier because he truly loved chocolate. "Save us a morsel of yourself." She laughed. "First, I must think of my young friend's good health. He's going to be a doctor." She leaned a bit more heavily on Daniel's arm.

The chocolatier patted his round stomach. "You skip the lunch," he advised. "It's chocolate that makes you strong."

Before the bus accident, Elise had not often gone to restaurants, preferring simple meals of tomato soup and toast. But in the past few years she'd grown fond of eating out. She liked saying "water" or "tea" or "check" and having the item delivered to her table by a smiling young person. At André's she'd become a familiar face; she'd made friends.

The sign in front of the restaurant said: PLEASE WAIT TO BE SEATED, but since the hostess was away, Elise led Daniel through the closely spaced tables.

"*Voilà!*" Elise whispered. Gertrude sat at the far end of the room, reading, fork hovering over a piece of yellow cake.

"Shall we ask her to join us?" asked Daniel.

Elise sat at a table with a view of Gertrude. "Let's wait to see what she does." Fork in hand, Gertrude turned a page. The cake looked untouched, and Elise wondered what kind it was—was it sponge cake? Whatever Gertrude was eating, Elise would pay for it. She would buy Gertrude's lunch, and Gertrude would be grateful.

Daniel stood beside the table. "Do you think she knows you're here?" he asked.

"She knows."

He looked at Gertrude, then back at Elise. "It seems funny, you sitting here and her over there."

Elise patted Daniel's hand. "Sit," she said. "We'll eat."

Once seated, Daniel's hands went to the container of white and pink packets, real and fake sugar. "Last year my mother and my sister had a terrible fight, and my sister ran away for two weeks. She took a bus to San Diego. I guess I know how it can be for a mother and a daughter, sort of ugly, even though you love each other." Daniel unfolded the menu in front of him, flapping the laminated pages.

27

"We'll get the special," said Elise. "It's always good."

A waitress maneuvered through the tables, loaded down with dishes. A bottle of ketchup poked out of her apron pocket. "We're ready," said Elise.

"In a minute." The waitress hurried to another table and began to dole out plates. When they had all been unloaded, the girl folded her arms and surveyed the scene. She pressed her forearms with her hands, kneading the muscles gently, like a delicate pastry dough.

Across the table, Daniel sat quietly, and Elise noticed that his hair was brown. "Where did you get that hair?" she asked. "I thought Chinese hair was black."

"It must be from being in the sun, playing tennis. Maybe it's from eating at McDonald's."

"Does your grandmother have small feet?"

Daniel smiled. "I never noticed."

Elise glanced over at Gertrude, at the piece of cake. It was just like Gertrude to order cake and then not eat it, to sit primly, back straight, legs crossed. She was wearing pale pink tights, a color that was charming for a girl but ludicrous for a sixty-year-old woman. If Elise complained, Gertrude would just say, "These are my work clothes."

"Hi, I'm Sandy."

Elise jerked her head, surprised to find the waitress inches away. The girl had one foot placed awkwardly in front of the other, almost as if she was pointing it.

"The special?" Daniel prompted.

"Not yet." Elise motioned discreetly toward Gertrude. "Do you see that lady with the pink legs? What kind of cake does she have?"

Sandy squinted toward Gertrude's table. She walked a few steps closer, then walked back. "Lemon."

"Thank you," said Elise. "We'll have the special."

Still the lemon cake sat undisturbed. Elise watched Gertrude's fork, thinking of the man she had seen on TV who stared at a spoon until it curled into itself. She stared at Gertrude, willing the fork to sink into the cake. But she felt Gertrude pushing up, against her downward gaze.

Gertrude was the one who had resisted reconciliation, the one who held a grudge. Elise had tried. It had been late in December, after the bus money was snug in a savings account at Mark Twain Bank. Elise had not seen Gertrude for several months, but it was Christmas, the season of families and love. Early in December, Elise had prepared little gifts for her neighbors and helpers—dates stuffed with almonds, rolled in sugar—and several boxes remained, stacked on the kitchen table. She decided to make a delivery.

Elise bundled up, pulled on her galoshes, tucked the foil-wrapped gift under her arm, and stepped outside. Clean snow blanketed the sidewalks and piled inside the empty swimming pool at the Oasis Apartments next door. In the street, cars had churned the snow into mush. Along the curb, the white drifts were freckled black. Elise plunged through snow and slush, across Brookside to the Beechwood Apartments. During the holiday season, the building glowed blue with Christmas lights; in daylight the strings looked like vines, the unilluminated bulbs like bitter fruit. Inside, the corridors were brightly lit, festooned with strands of garland, and many of the doors had wreaths. Elise knocked on Gertrude's door.

"Well," said Gertrude. "Hello." She stood in the doorway in a light blue jogging suit and her stocking feet. Her hair hung down her back in one long braid.

"Merry Christmas, Gertrude," said Elise.

"You're brave to come out in all that snow."

"I like snow," said Elise.

The women stood facing each other without saying anything.

"I've always liked snow," said Elise.

"Would you like to come in?"

Nothing in Gertrude's apartment matched, but it all fit together, bright colors and bold patterns, scarves and fringed pillows. The rooms seemed out of place in a retirement community. Elise, timid among such exuberance, kept her fingers curled tightly around the dates.

A big book called *Yoga with Judy* lay on Gertrude's coffee table. "What in the world?" said Elise. "You're learning to hypnotize people?"

"You've heard of yoga," said Gertrude. "It's for meditating and relaxing. It has nothing to do with hypnosis." Gertrude had swung her braid over her shoulder. As a little girl, she had sucked on the ends of her hair. Now she was pulling on it, stroking it like a pet. "What are you holding there?" she asked.

Elise thrust the shiny box at Gertrude. "Dates."

"How nice! I haven't had one of these for about a hundred years." While Gertrude plucked at the foil wrap, Elise examined the other items on the coffee table. She flipped through a stack of large black-and-white photos that showed Gertrude with students. The students were doing basic ballet exercises, pliés and stretches at the barre. But there was something in their poses, something floppy and off-balance.

"One of the mothers gave me those," said Gertrude. "She called the newspaper, and the photographer sent the prints."

Elise studied a picture of four girls and one boy, each stretching one leg back in an ungainly arabesque. "Like jellyfish," said Elise. "No muscles."

"That's my special class. Didn't you see my picture last Sunday?" She handed Elise a newspaper folded open to the society page. The most prominent photo showed Brice and Allen Antioch at a holiday party, each gripping a sequined wife with one hand, a drink with the other. The picture warmed her, and she remembered them as boys, when she had been their nanny. Elise had seen this picture already—she'd been pleased to see her boys having fun—but she hadn't looked farther down the page. Other pictures showed black debutantes, giggly and glamorous in long dresses. Then, at the bottom of the page, under the headline, "Special Nutcracker," was a picture of Gertrude and the wobbly children.

Elise stared at the picture, mortified. They were mongoloid children. Gertrude was teaching mongoloids. Elise dropped the paper to the floor and wiped her fingers on her coat. It was horrible. She thought of Brice and Allen's reaction when they saw Gertrude's picture; she could imagine them laughing and laughing. She gathered up the foil that Gertrude had ripped from the box. She pressed the pieces into a tight ball and put it in her pocket. At home she would try to fashion a usable sheet out of the scraps. Gertrude could keep the dates—Elise had more boxes than she could use or give away already. But Elise would take back the foil; she would take back the box. "You'll have to get something for these," she blurted. "I need that box."

Gertrude brought a plate from the kitchen and began unpacking the dates one by one.

Elise watched, her face hot, her mind crowded with images of deformed dancers. She grabbed the box. "Don't be so fussy, Gertrude. They're not glass." She turned the box upside down, scattering sugar in a brief, gritty blizzard. Several dates bounced off the plate and stuck on the table like squashed bugs.

Elise tucked the emptied box back under her arm. She took a date and held it in her fingers, pressing into the sticky softness. She wanted to slap Gertrude. She wanted to tell her not to walk around in her socks. "Thank you for helping the whole city to laugh at me," she said. "Thank you for that lovely Christmas gift."

In the bright corridor, she ate the date, hardly noticing its sweetness, although she felt the grains of sugar against her teeth. When she got outside, she cleaned her hands in the snow.

Walking home, Elise worked the foil wad with her fingers, pressing it tighter, harder, smaller. A cloying aftertaste hung in her mouth, a sickening taste of decay, of shame.

When Elise focused again on Gertrude's yellow cake, something seemed different. Gertrude had taken a bite. Elise took a deep breath; she stood and walked to Gertrude's table.

"How do you like the lemon cake, Gertrude?"

Gertrude looked up, her face calm. "Fine, Mother."

From so close, Elise could see the uneven surface of the frosting, where the knife had made dips and swirls. She wanted to shove her finger in. If I'm going to pay, she thought, I'm entitled.

"Was there something you wanted to say to me?" said Gertrude.

"Do you mind if I take a taste? I might buy a piece if I like it."

For a second it seemed that Gertrude hadn't heard, then she pushed the plate over. Elise picked a bit off the edge where the tines of the fork had made a jagged imprint. The crumb was so small it dissolved in her mouth; she could hardly get any taste from it, just a tiny tingle, a lemony pinprick.

The paperback book had fallen closed in Gertrude's hand. The title, *Zen and the Art of Motorcycle Maintenance,* didn't surprise Elise. Nothing about Gertrude surprised her, not even a book about motorcycle repair.

"In China," said Elise, "daughters respect their mothers. In China you would be a disgrace."

"Mmm," said Gertrude.

"You see," Elise said, pointing at Daniel. "Chinese."

"Yes."

"Answer me," Elise demanded.

Gertrude put down her fork. She folded her hands on the table, crossed her pale pink ankles. She said, "You haven't asked a question."

"I was nearly crushed by a bus," said Elise.

"Is that a question?"

"Don't make jokes. I could have died."

Gertrude nodded. "But you didn't."

Elise thought of smashing her fist into the cake, watching Gertrude's face crumple. "Tell me one thing, Gertrude—why should I buy this cake for you? Why should I?"

"There's no reason. I don't want you to."

"I have friends, Gertrude. Both young and old."

Walking back to Daniel's table, Elise heard Gertrude's voice, quiet but clear: "Then you must be very happy."

When the quiche came, Elise wasn't hungry. She ate bits of ham and left the custard.

"Why do you follow her around if it upsets you?" asked Daniel.

"I'm not following her. I'm living my life."

"Wouldn't it be easier to avoid her?"

"Gertrude is the one who is following me. She's the one who moved in at the Beechwood Apartments." Daniel nodded. He looked concerned. Elise liked him; he was so understanding and attentive. "You know, Daniel, we could make this a sort of ongoing appointment. I could treat you to lunch every Saturday. I could be your replacement granny."

"I'd like that," said Daniel. "I would. Except that most Saturdays, I go cycling. But thanks. Thank you."

Elise knew he was lying by the way he stuttered. "How about another day?"

"I'd like to, but I have so much studying, huge amounts."

"You'll be old, too," she said, not caring if it made him feel bad. It was nothing but the truth. She gathered her belongings—pocketbook, scarf. "We'll split this one down the middle, shall we?"

Daniel cleared his throat. "To tell you the truth, I don't have any cash on me. Let me call Alex and have him bring some money."

Elise let Daniel push his chair back, let him stand, before she laughed. "I'm teasing," she said. "Didn't I tell you this was my treat?"

"I don't want to force you. I'll call Alex."

"I was joking," said Elise. "Joking."

At the cash register, Elise paid with a hundred-dollar bill. She liked big bills, enjoyed hearing the little gasps when she handed them to clerks. She got seven or eight of them out of the bank at once, to save herself time.

Elise chatted loudly with the cashier, as if Gertrude would bother to eavesdrop. Daniel was at her side, quiet as a bodyguard. Behind the counter, the fat chocolatier was straightening the candy.

Standing at the cash register, waiting for her change, Elise was overwhelmed by exhaustion. Her body was no longer hair and toenails and veins; her body had become an accumulation of aches. She took Daniel's arm, felt him stiffen his muscles to support her weight.

"Miss?" called the chocolatier as Elise turned to go. "Excuse me, miss." He motioned her toward the counter, then handed her a small object wrapped in shiny red paper. "A chocolate walnut," he said. "Because you are sweet."

*E*lise spread the Sunday paper on the kitchen table and worked her way through. She read more carefully now, more warily, but Gertrude's notoriety had not been repeated. Brice and Allen Antioch, on the other hand, smiled at her from the society pages almost every week. When Elise turned seventy, Brice and Allen had surprised her with a retirement dinner. The biggest part of the surprise was the retirement itself; Elise had expected to work until she was no longer able to. She hadn't outlived her usefulness once the boys grew up. She'd taken on other household responsibilities, like ironing and answering the phone.

At the retirement dinner, they ate on the Antiochs' finest china, on the tablecloth Elise had ironed that afternoon. The cook prepared lamb with mint sauce, baby carrots, new potatoes, and lemon soufflé. Gertrude, invited as part of the surprise, had embarrassed Elise terribly. Brice and Allen gave Elise a gold brooch and behaved marvelously; Gertrude wore slacks and refused to eat the meat. And she'd picked fights, blaming the boys for things that were not their fault, sticking her nose where it didn't belong.

"What do you think happens when a business moves out of downtown?" Gertrude had asked, elbows on the table.

Elise shot furious looks at Gertrude, who ignored her. The Antiochs didn't discuss business at dinner—Gertrude knew that. And they certainly didn't raise their voices. As Gertrude got louder, Brice's voice dropped to a murmur.

"The energy of the city is in Overland Park," Brice stated calmly. "That's a fact, Gertrude, I can't stop it. It made *sense* to move to Overland Park—I *live* in Overland Park."

"It's the little businesses that suffer," said Gertrude, "the ones that can't afford to move."

"This is business, Gertrude. We can't worry about how our decisions might affect every wig store and dance studio on the block."

"Of course not. And don't worry either about how every empty building makes downtown less safe."

Brice laughed. "So basically, if a ballerina gets mugged, it will be on my conscience."

Allen coughed softly. "Brice, Gertrude, I think a truce is in order. I propose a toast." He raised his wineglass. "To Elise, who loved us like a mother."

Elise lifted her glass daintily. "To the Antiochs. To my boys."

Elise had refused to speak to Gertrude until they were past the doorman, outside the Antiochs' apartment building. Then she spat words out angrily. "I have never been so ashamed. You know perfectly well how to behave, and you refuse to do so."

"I know how to behave," said Gertrude. "But I will not curtsey to the Antiochs' lemon soufflé. Those boys make me sick. You work there for forty years, and they give you a week's notice and a snooty dinner. No pension, nothing."

Elise spoke in a restrained, precise voice. "This was my dinner. The dinner in my honor, and you ruined it with your ugly talk and bad manners." She felt tears rising, but she pushed them down. She didn't need Gertrude; she had Brice and Allen. They weren't her sons, but they loved her. She could count on them.

After that Elise had made no effort to see Gertrude, and years went by. Gertrude sent money every week, but since the checks were for differing amounts, it was difficult for Elise to rely on them. Brice and Allen didn't send money, but Elise wore their pin on her coat and felt their love. After the bus accident, she had asked the desk nurse to call Brice or Allen as her next of kin. But they were both abroad, and Gertrude came instead.

Elise finished the paper and folded it. Sunday was a day so long and empty she could practically hear it flapping in the wind. The Antiochs had entertained on Sunday afternoons—leisurely parties with strawberries and champagne. Elise had been there sometimes, looking after the children. She decided that if anyone dropped in today, she would excuse herself into the bathroom and pinch her cheeks to make herself feel less drab.

On Monday Elise was restless. She considered taking a walk, but the weather was chilly, and she didn't really feel up to it. She used to walk around Loose Park quite frequently, but lately she was afraid of getting stranded. She didn't like the park as much as she used to anyway, not since the city installed a fountain in the middle of the duck pond. And she was uncomfortable with the number of black people who walked or jogged along the path. Loose Park seemed less and less like her park, and more and more like a park for anyone.

Elise walked from kitchen to living room to bedroom and back again, searching the floor for lint. She stepped into the hall, but she didn't expect anyone to be around on a weekday. She heard nothing at all, then, faintly, a typewriter downstairs, Alex or Daniel.

She could read or listen to the radio or turn on the television, but none of these sounded interesting. She thought of calling down to Alex and Daniel's apartment and asking who was typing. It didn't seem healthy to study so much. If they were doctors, they should know that too many books and typewriters could strain the eyes.

Elise didn't normally eat sweets, but she recalled a blueberry muffin mix tucked in the back of her cupboard. Brice and Allen had always clamored after cookies and cupcakes. She would bake and open the door wide and wait to see if any boys floated up from downstairs.

She took the box from the shelf, slit the cardboard with a knife. Inside was a sealed plastic bag of mix and a small can of wild blueberries. She poured the mix into a bowl, added water, oil, egg, then reached for the blueberries. But when she attached the can opener to the rim, she found that she couldn't squeeze with enough force to pierce the tin. She leaned her arm on the lever. But the opener slipped, nicking the skin on her wrist.

Taking the can and the opener, she went down the stairs. Once she had given Alex a can of green beans to open. Elise knocked softly on Alex and Daniel's door; she heard typing—the clatter of keys and the occasional ding of the carriage return. "Yoo-hoo," she called. "Alex? Daniel?" No one answered. She stood in the dim corridor, holding the can; the label showed tiny blueberries the color of dusk. The bulb overhead had burned out, and Elise felt uneasy, even though she was in her own building. Alone in the darkness, she thought of the bus accident, felt the lurch, the turning and tumbling in her stomach; she waited for the crunch of bones. She remembered the concrete scratching against her neck and the strange cushion her bun had made, as if she were using a dinner roll for a pillow. She turned the can. Flat, paper berries spilled into her hand. She knocked harder. Nothing.

She rode downtown in a soiled cab, watched busy people rushing by. Brush Creek trickled innocently, deceptively, within its cement banks, a dribble of dirty water; nearby buildings still showed marks from the flood. At Forty-seventh, the horse fountain galloped by, already shut off for the winter.

At the door of the brown brick building, Elise hesitated, clutching the blueberries. It would take Gertrude less than a minute to open the can. Not even Gertrude could refuse. She pulled open the heavy door. Inside, a narrow stairway led up to a glass door with black letters: STAR GLAMOUR DANCE STUDIO. The stairs were speckled marble, pink and beige; at the center of each step, Elise could see an indentation where the marble had worn away. If she went up, she'd find a big, bare room, a wooden floor with dust along the edges. She'd seen enough dance studios to know that they were all the same—piano, mirrors, rosin, benches, students, mothers. She would not go up. She would not sit on a bench beside the mother of a mongoloid, watching Gertrude tilt heads and lift rib cages, watching Gertrude dance. She would wait for Gertrude to come down.

Framed recital photographs lined the walls—tap dancers in sequins and top hats, ballerinas of all ages. When Gertrude was just out of her teens, she'd been in the chorus of several shows in New York City, but on the wall in the stairwell there were no pictures of Gertrude dancing.

At the top of the stairs, the door opened, then closed. Elise moved closer to the wall, pretending to study the photos. Her body tensed, anticipating an onslaught of mongoloid children. They would engulf her, pummel her with ballet slippers. Elise glanced nervously upward, toward the door, where Gertrude stood waiting.

"We seem to be leading parallel lives," said Gertrude.

"I don't know about that," Elise said, confused and somewhat comforted by Gertrude's pink legs. She watched her daughter descend. At the bottom, Gertrude pushed the street door, and they stepped into the open air.

"What are you doing here, Mother?"

Elise held up the can of blueberries. "I can't open this." In her hand the can surprised her; it seemed so small and harmless. "I was making muffins." She pushed the can toward Gertrude.

"I don't understand. Do you want me to open it?"

Elise held the can and looked at the label, at its promise of plump sweetness and blue juice. She liked the way the tin held the berries in place. "No," she said. "Take it."

"I don't really want it."

"I want you to have it."

Gertrude kept her hands in the pockets of her overcoat. "This is my bus," she said.

Elise looked up to see a massive tire, an enormous bus. She took a step back, holding tight to the blueberries. The bus, camouflaged by soot, had snuck up on her. But she could see through the dirt to the black-and-white stripes below. Elise wondered if the pattern was authentic, if an actual zebra had posed while the artist traced and painted. Looking closely at the zoo bus, she noticed that the lines were blurred, the borders uncertain. The white stripes were dingy; the black stripes were gray. The door opened with a groan, and Gertrude stepped in. Elise glanced from side to side to see if anyone was watching, then she lifted her foot to reach the step; clutching the railing on both sides, she hoisted herself up.

The driver wore a blue uniform with rolled-up sleeves. Elise expected to see him in khaki shorts and a safari hat. She expected to hear parrots and sultry tropical music. Gertrude tossed some change into the rattling metal money counter at the front of the bus. The door closed with a sigh, bureaucratic and indifferent.

"I'll pay for both of ours," said Elise.

"She already paid," said the driver.

Elise opened her billfold and pulled out her money—three hundred-dollar bills. She handed him one. "For mine."

"Can't change that. Exact change only." The driver's blue cap rested on the dashboard. He put it on, pulling at its slick black bill.

Elise raised her voice. "Will a hundred-dollar bill collapse our city's economy?"

"Put that away," said the driver. "Before someone knocks you down and snatches it. The other lady already paid for you."

"She had no right to pay for me."

"Listen, I have a schedule. Either sit down or get off."

Standing at the front of the bus, looking back, Elise felt as if she was about to enter a tin of sardines. Gertrude had taken a seat just past the middle of the bus, but Elise wasn't sure she wanted to sit there. She didn't want to sit beside a stranger either—someone who might turn out to be a criminal or a lunatic. The passengers sat with coats buttoned to their necks, shopping bags nestled at their feet, but years of riding the buses had taught her that there were no guarantees.

It would be best, Elise decided, to sit with Gertrude. She walked toward her daughter, grasping the metal headrests. She felt Gertrude's calm eyes but avoided looking into them—she didn't want to be hypnotized. Gertrude might be an expert by now.

Elise sat, the money folded in her fist. In the seat ahead, a baby in a yellow knit cap peeped over its mother's shoulder. The baby grimaced, then grinned, then began to cry. Elise jabbed the money toward Gertrude. "Take it, then."

Gertrude's straight back barely touched the seat. Her hands, folded in her lap, were pale and freckled and wrinkled. "I don't want it."

"How much did you put in? Take what you put in and give me the change." Elise tried to drop the money into Gertrude's lap, but it fluttered to the floor.

Reaching to retrieve the bill, Gertrude whispered in Elise's ear.

"Put your money away." Then, upright, in a more normal tone, she said, "You have to be careful. People kill other people for a bag of hamburgers."

"I don't want you to pay." Elise tried to push the money into Gertrude's hand again, but Gertrude wouldn't close her fingers around the bill.

"Really, Mother, it's my treat." She put her finger out for the baby to play with. "You're a sweet baby," she cooed. "Aren't you a sweet baby?"

Elise wanted to take Gertrude's finger out of the baby's grasp and put her own in. She wanted to touch the tiny fingernails, the little pompon on its cap.

"I had the toddler class this morning," said Gertrude. "Eight little girls in tap shoes, very noisy. I'm getting too old for this."

"I could give you the whole hundred dollars," said Elise.

"I don't want your money."

Elise looked Gertrude straight in the face. "Don't you see? I can help you. I can put you in my will—I can give you money now. All you have to do is ask."

"I don't need it," Gertrude said firmly.

Silent, Elise sat and watched Gertrude shake her finger free of the baby's grasp. Elise wanted to grab Gertrude's finger and give it a twist. "You would want it well enough if no one was watching. You would help yourself—don't pretend you wouldn't."

"If you say so," said Gertrude. She reached up and pulled the wire that snaked around the bus above the windows. A sharp buzz sounded at the front of the bus.

"This isn't our stop."

"I'm getting out here." She gazed steadily at Elise, who looked away. "I'm sorry, but whatever it is you want from me—I don't have it."

"I don't want anything from you. I'm trying to give you something."

"Excuse me," said Gertrude.

Elise felt panicky; she held tightly to her purse. "I'm just trying to give you the bus fare. I'm trying to give you what I owe."

"When you get to the street before your house, pull the cord, and the driver will let you out. You remember." Gertrude edged past. She stood straight and walked away, tall and proud, like an African woman in a documentary, able to carry baskets in each hand while balancing another on her head. Once she was off the bus, Gertrude stood on the sidewalk, facing the street. She was looking toward the bus, as if waiting for something else to happen.

Well, good-bye to you, thought Elise. Good-bye to Gertrude. Good riddance. She watched the baby in front of her. As the bus pulled away from the curb, the baby's head rolled from side to side, its neck flexible, unformed. Such a small baby—it was too early to know whether it would be sickly or ugly or mean. That tiny, lumpy package, that baby, could hold a lifetime of bitterness and hate.

The world through the window grew dim, day dissolving into darkness, and the zoo bus rolled along down Broadway. Elise wondered where the bus would take her if she rode it to the end, if she'd end up at the zoo. If it were earlier in the day, she would do just that— throw marshmallows at the elephants and ride a camel. She imagined walking through the zoo, pausing to look at a patch of pink, a flock of flamingos. There, at the edge of the lagoon, standing on one pink leg, was Gertrude.

Ridiculous. Gertrude was ridiculous. No one could love her.

Elise reached her hand out to the baby, but it didn't notice; its head was burrowed into the mother's shoulder. A circle of spit darkened the material of the mother's dress. Elise touched the baby's face with her finger and felt warm skin that was so soft it frightened her. The baby's eyelids opened halfway at her touch then closed heavily.

When Gertrude was a baby she had slept in a drawer, but it was a drawer that Elise had removed from the dresser and placed on the floor. She would never have done what Alex suggested, closing the drawer with a baby inside. She would never do that. Elise had made the drawer into a cozy nest, and Gertrude had slept comfortably. Each night before bedtime Elise's husband, Bill, had filled a big mixing bowl with warm water and soapsuds. His hands were thick and oil stained, and they colored the bath water brown. But he loved to wash his baby, loved to dribble water from the washcloth onto her belly. Elise closed her eyes. She could see the dark-haired man, the dark-haired baby, the kitchen table, herself. She stood by the stove, watching Bill and the baby, waiting for the flatiron to heat; her long hair was tied back with a ribbon.

When Elise opened her eyes, she was sitting in a bus that smelled of exhaust and sour milk. She tasted salt on her lips. She wanted to rush to the back of the bus and press herself against the window, push backward through time and space as the bus rolled ahead. She wrapped her hands around the metal headrest of the seat in front of her and tried to stand, but the bus lurched beneath her feet, and she was standing and kneeling and clutching the seat.

Now? she thought. Would he love her now—a grown woman in pink tights? Would he love Gertrude now?

She called out to the driver, but her voice was swallowed up by the roar of the engine. A young man in a tan overcoat reached up and pulled the cord.

When the bus came to a stop, Elise stood and made her way to the front. All around her the passengers were goggle-eyed, like fish. She thought of the wobbly children in Gertrude's photographs, the awkward poses and soggy flesh. Her hands curled into fists. But if she saw the children in person, if she saw them dance ... She thought of watching Gertrude's early dance lessons, many years ago. Gertrude had practiced past awkwardness and uncertainty, her movements becoming so fluid, so flexible that Elise had been tempted to press against her daughter's skin and feel for bones.

Standing at the edge of the bus steps, Elise caught her breath. The steps were steep as a precipice, and they led into darkness; she wavered at the top, afraid of falling. But by sitting down on the step, she made her way, pressing her fingers against the black rubber treads, scooting one stair at a time.

She was on Broadway, somewhere in midtown—she wasn't sure where. In front of her an auto dealership displayed hundreds of parked cars, prices painted on the windshields. An endless string of plastic flags—brightly colored triangles—marked the border of the lot.

She could find Gertrude still. She could go to her. Slowly, Elise began walking, moving toward where Gertrude had been, navigating by the plastic flags that flapped and fretted in the wind.

YOU'RE SO BEAUTIFUL

ood-bye," said Sydney, testing the silence. "I'm all alone."
She pretended there was an echo in the car, "Alone . . . alone . . .
alone . . ." Her voice sounded strange, hoarse. She cleared her throat.
Her parents would be gone for almost two months, on a "South Sea
Odyssey." At Christmas they would show up, sporting leathery,
tanned skin and carrying piles of worthless presents—coconut bras
and dolls in native costumes, foreign candies that were too sweet and
cookies that weren't sweet at all. Early in December, Sydney was supposed to lug the artificial tree down from the attic, and the box of decorations, the tangle of balding garland, and make the house
Christmasy.

Overhead, the traffic signs loomed: St. Louis, Des Moines, Wichita.
Perhaps the highway would pick a destination and just send her there,
spit her out at exits and interchanges until she ran out of gas somewhere in Iowa. She watched the green signs rush up, then rush past—
Exit A—Exit B—.

"Molly and Frank have both promised to check in on you," her mother had assured her.

Molly. Sure. Sydney knew exactly what Molly would do: "Hi, can you baby-sit Friday, Saturday, and Sunday?" And Molly thought it was an insult to pay a family member for baby-sitting—an insult to the person who spent all night changing diapers!

"Don't worry, honey," her mother had said. "You're a big girl. You're sixteen."

"I'm not worried," Sydney had said. "You're the one that sounds worried."

"I trust you. Frank will come home most weekends to see how you're doing. And you have our itinerary, so you can get in touch with us if you need to. You're lucky to have a brother and sister living nearby."

Sydney wished Frank would hurry up and graduate—and move far away. He was in his fifth year at KU, but he'd changed his major so many times he wouldn't graduate for at least another year. The last Sydney had heard he was studying Personnel, whatever that was.

With one hand on the wheel, Sydney slipped her other hand into her sweater pocket and touched the layers of tissue that protected her good luck charm. Last week, at the end of the dissecting unit in Biology II, she had cut the ear off Myrtle, her fetal pig. Some of the boys in the class had pretended to eat pieces of their pigs, but Sydney was the only person who had actually taken a piece out of the biology room. She had liked the way the ear felt, soft and silky. And she'd thought a pig ear might prove useful.

When Sydney had showed the ear to her friends, they screamed and pushed their chairs away from the lunch table. "There's no reason to get hysterical," she told them, wrapping up the ear, hiding it away. "It's like leather. You're not afraid of a football, are you?"

Now a big, junky car roared past on the right; Sydney grabbed hold of the steering wheel with both hands. She thought of the Vietnam vet who had visited her history class when she was a freshman—he had gone to her school years before. He told the students that some soldiers liked to cut off the ears of dead Vietcong. He said he had a boxful of ears at home. The man was thirty years old and wore ragged army pants and plastic pool thongs; Sydney thought he might be crazy. After the class, Sydney wanted to ask the teacher, "Was he always like that?"

Benton Boulevard. Southwest Trafficway. Sydney took a chance on Paseo and found her way somehow, past stores with barred windows and yards enclosed by chain link fences.

At home, she pulled the bolt on the front door, then got a glass out of the kitchen and poured an inch of whiskey from one of her parents' big bottles. If anyone asked, she would say that Frank drank it. That was one benefit of being the youngest child—no one ever suspected her of anything, not that she did much of anything suspicious. Nothing more than a few sips of whiskey every month or two. Sydney sat on the couch with her feet on the coffee table, drained of all energy. She scanned the mantle and the bookshelves, looking at the dolls her parents had collected on trips throughout the years. Even as a little girl she had hated the dolls, their tiny plastic faces, their stiff, ludicrous costumes. Voodoo dolls. She wanted to stick pins in them.

Sydney gathered a handful off the nearest shelf. She tried to guess each nationality, then checked the label on the underside of the stand: Scotland, Turkey, Iran, France, Belgium. Scotland was the only one she got right; the kilt and bagpipe gave that one away. Growing up, Sydney had never been allowed to touch her parents' dolls. But she'd had her trusty American dolls—My Beautiful Chrissie and, of course, Barbie. She tried to remember what she'd done with dolls. What was so fun about them? She remembered orchestrating dates and weddings. Barbie would marry Ken, and they would drive to Colorado and climb a mountain and then have dinner in the nicest restaurant. Then Sydney would take off the dolls' clothes and leave them together in a shoebox, her own face flushing, her body prickling with curiosity and shame.

When had she stopped playing with dolls? Sydney took a sip of whiskey and pretended to ponder the idea, but she knew exactly when—she knew it was the summer before sixth grade, the summer Nicole Lefferson vanished.

Fairway—where Sydney lived—was a suburb of Kansas City, but safe and clean like a small town. Elm trees lined the streets and people kept their sidewalks swept. In the summer, children stayed outside past dark, playing ghosts in the graveyard, and murder, and boo!—games designed to frighten, though no one was ever truly scared.

Fairway was safe and clean, and then Nicole disappeared one day in the middle of the afternoon as she walked home from the swimming pool. Nicole's brother, Patrick, had been with her, ahead of her; they were racing, he said later. A spurt of speed, a whoop of victory, a glance back, and she was gone.

Slouched on the sofa, glass balanced on her chest, Sydney tried to remember everything she could about Nicole Lefferson—Nicole had been a year younger, so Sydney didn't know her well. But the Leffersons had a trampoline in the backyard, and once, early that summer, Nicole had asked Sydney over. Nicole had tried to set a record that day for a maneuver called the tabletop, a kind of horizontal pivot, and she had Sydney keep count. She taught Sydney how to do a knee flip and then a front flip. When they were both tired, panting in the heat, Nicole brought out two cans of Shasta grapefruit soda. Sydney had been amazed at that—her own mother never bought soda. She remembered that Nicole would say "That's so queer" whenever she thought something was silly. She remembered a bright green dress that Nicole used to wear at church.

Patrick Lefferson was in Sydney's class in school. Handsome and tragic, he was one of the boys that the girls all fantasized about. He had hardly spoken a word since the day Nicole disappeared. Once, playing soccer during recess, he ran smash into one of the high stone walls that surrounded the playground. The girls had cried and swarmed around, watching the blood dripping down his forehead. Every girl prayed that he would ask her to sit beside him in the nurse's office, to hold his hand while he was being bandaged.

Of course that never happened. But at the graduation party in eighth grade, Patrick had asked Sydney to dance. She'd been so nervous at the party, so giggly and chatty. She had been telling him about a newspaper article she'd read: a horse had been stuck in its stable for three years, and the manure had piled up, three years' worth. The picture that ran alongside the article showed the horse standing in a clean stable, healthy and happy now, except that his hooves had grown up, up, like renegade toenails.

"It looked like a new kind of animal," she said. "Like part elf and part horse. Do you want some gum?"

Patrick took a piece, then asked her to dance. He held her close, sunk his hands into her fuzzy white lambswool sweater, the one she'd gotten at the flood sale at Fashion Gal.

"Soft," he said, and he pulled her closer, their bodies touching like they were hugging. "You Light Up My Life" was playing on the stereo. Sydney clasped her hands behind his neck. When the song ended, he asked her to dance again. But as they waited for the music, a piece of fluff had floated from the sweater and landed in her eye. Sydney had had to rush to the bathroom and splash water into her eye, then she stayed in there, crying, because—she wasn't sure why. Because she was dancing with Patrick Lefferson, and then she wasn't anymore.

Patrick had ended up going to a different high school, and Sydney rarely saw him now. Nicole's body was discovered a week after the graduation party. A farmer found her bones, her plastic hair barrettes, in a ditch in Salina, Kansas. For the two years since she had disappeared, the students at St. Bernadette's had prayed for Nicole every morning—that she was in a good place, that she knew they were thinking of her. And Sydney always hoped, believed, that they would find her. Nicole's bones. Sydney couldn't mesh Nicole's bones with Nicole's green dress. Nicole with her hand around a can of grapefruit soda. Nicole on the trampoline, gasping, "Water, water," her tongue hanging out, like a dog in the desert. When the bones were found, Sydney cried again, cried and cried.

Sydney laid the dolls side by side on the coffee table. When she was younger, she used to wonder what they did at night. Maybe they all joined up hands and taught each other folk dances, humming the tunes in sweet, stupid doll voices. Maybe they snuck into her room and stood beside her bed and watched her sleep.

She took her empty glass to the kitchen and rinsed it, let the water run a long time, warm water washing over her wrists, her palms, her knuckles. She thought of calling a friend or calling Molly—just to touch voices with another person—but she felt so tired she went to her room instead, lay down on her bed with her clothes on. Tomorrow was Friday and Frank would be home. In the morning, she would try to move her dresser; she would see if she was strong enough to push it in front of her door. She fell asleep with her hand in her pocket, her fingers resting on the wad of tissue, the small, soft lump of Myrtle's ear.

Carmen wanted to double with Sydney to the winter formal. "You can still go if no one asks you. Ask a boy from another school." Carmen smoothed the pleats on her drill team uniform, pulled up her knee socks, and folded over the tops.

Sydney took her hairbrush out of her locker, then put it back. Drill team members weren't supposed to brush their hair in public. If someone saw her, she would get half a point. The drill team rules—fifteen pages' worth—were strict, but not unreasonable. Sydney thought they accomplished their purpose, which was to help the team keep up a classy image. Even the weigh-ins made sense: if a girl was fat, the audience might laugh at her. And what was the point of practicing so hard if the members were going to go around looking like slobs? Who would want to watch them if the group got a reputation for being sleazy or vain?

"Who could you ask?" pressed Carmen. "Think."

"If no one asks me," said Sydney, "I don't want to go."

"Don't be such a girl."

"I am a girl."

Every day for a month Carmen had come to school full of plans and ideas for the dance. She wanted them to make dinner—a Mexican theme or Italian or maybe just steaks. Guys loved red meat. She had some idea from *Seventeen* for using aluminum foil in her hair and painting an old pair of tap shoes silver. The night before the dance, they would deep-condition their hair and give themselves avocado-egg facials and glue on fake fingernails. The night of the dance they would wear strapless bras and strapless gowns and be kissed romantically on their doorsteps.

Now Carmen stood at the locker looking perturbed, forehead wrinkled, eyebrows bunched.

Sydney tossed out a name. "Maybe Patrick Lefferson," she said. "This boy from St. B's. You remember Nicole Lefferson? Did you read about her in the paper?"

"The girl from the swimming pool? The girl who got"—Carmen whispered the last part—"killed?"

"It's her brother."

Carmen looked doubtful. "Maybe you better not."

"Why not?"

"I don't know. What if he's damaged? Try to think of someone else. Think."

But Sydney couldn't think of the winter formal at all. She couldn't think of Patrick Lefferson. All she could think of were Frank's footsteps across her beautiful blue plush carpet. Slow and sneaky, like a cat padding across a lawn. Her dresser weighed much too much, even when she took the drawers out. She couldn't budge it. But when she piled the drawers up against the door, they weren't solid enough to stop someone from coming in.

One night last summer, Sydney had awakened to find Frank standing beside her bed. She had felt his hand on her breast. Her T-shirt was pulled up, twisted. The sheet was on the floor. She felt the air from the fan on her belly. "What are you doing?" she asked.

"Nothing," he said, and his hand was gone; dissolved, subtracted. He fixed his eyes to hers. "Did you take money out of my wallet?"

"No."

"Well, someone did."

Sydney remembered what she did when he left; she got out of bed and put her clothes on. It was summer, but she put on jeans, underwear, bra, shirt, socks, then she lay in bed, pulled the sheet up over her. She didn't take his money. What money? His hand on her breast. What money? She felt sweat dampen her jeans, her shirt, the heavy fabric welding itself to her body. She stumbled in the darkness, found a sweatshirt, put it on.

The next morning Frank had acted exactly the same way he always acted, sloshing orange juice on the table, memorizing the sports page, making hums and grunts as he ate his Cheerios. Sydney's father was at work; her mother was doing laundry in the basement. Sydney took her toast and peanut butter and went into the living room to read the front part of the paper.

A minute or two later Frank came in holding the sports page. "You done with that part?" he asked. Sydney pushed it to him. He would take it whether she was done or not.

"I found my money," he said.

"Good for you," said Sydney.

Now Sydney rummaged in her locker, looking for her French book. Two months was eight weekends. Eight weekends with Frank. Eight postcards from her parents.

"Well?" said Carmen.

"Can I spend the night?" asked Sydney.

With drill team practice on Saturday afternoon and then work on Saturday night, Sydney didn't see Frank until Sunday morning. And when she finally did bump into him, he was perfectly nice. Sydney thought maybe he had gotten a girlfriend, or maybe somebody had punched him and told him to shape up. He even surprised her with a box of doughnuts when she got back from church—not just long johns, which were his favorite, but kinds she actually liked: coconuts and colored sprinkles and chocolate old-fashioneds.

Sydney scrambled eggs. Frank laid out plates and forks and napkins, and asked about her classes.

"Does Dumas still have that buzz cut?"

"He says, 'I have a short temper 'cause I'm a short-haired man.' " Sydney ran her hand over her head, imitating the geometry teacher.

"What an ass," said Frank. "I didn't learn a thing in his class."

" 'When you *assume* something, you make an ass of you and me.' "

"Does he still say that?"

"Every day," said Sydney. "Practically."

Sitting in the kitchen, eating doughnuts with Frank, Sydney remembered when she was six, when she was a cheerleader for Frank's seventh-grade football team. Her mother had made green yarn pompons for Sydney to wear on her shoes. Other little girls would stand with her and pretend to be cheerleaders, but they didn't have pompons on their shoes, and Sydney had been confident that they weren't nearly as cute. She remembered mud and grass, boys patting her on the head, Frank smiling.

But she also remembered coming home from school a hundred afternoons, settling into an episode of *The Brady Bunch* or *The Partridge Family*—then Frank would come in and change the channel. If Sydney ran to her mother, Frank would torture her by sitting through the whole program and making fun of the characters and the plot. He would call Mrs. Brady a bitch, or he would act like he wanted to have sex with Marsha or Jan or even Cindy. Once when he tried to change the channel, Sydney—nine or ten years old—had run at him, arms flailing, fists pounding, screaming, "Fucker!" That was the one time Frank had backed off. He said, "I'm going to call the funny farm," and he left the room, and she didn't see him again until dinner.

*A*s soon as Sydney had stepped one foot into the gray light of the community center basement, Mel spotted her and ran over. He was divorced and balding, with only tufts of hair sticking out from the sides; the top of his head was bright red. "We missed you last week," he said.

"I had to drive my parents to the airport." Sydney gave a stiff, polite smile. She didn't want him to follow her around all night. She disengaged a bent hanger from the coat rack and hung her jacket quickly, before he could make a big deal out of helping her.

Sydney's sister, Molly, had introduced Sydney to the folk dance club; Molly was the one who had seen the flyer on a grocery store bulletin board. But now that Molly had the baby, she never wanted to go. Carmen had come along a few times, but she wasn't very reliable. It was pointless to come infrequently. Each week the group worked on learning one or two new dances, and if you missed, you ended up turning in circles the next week, tripping, and staring desperately at other peoples' feet. Even though Mel pestered her, Sydney didn't want to give up the lessons. She loved learning the dances. For one thing, it was a good workout. And Sydney had fun dressing in sandals and full skirts and pretending to be a peasant dancing in a town square. She loved the stories some of the dances told, the men pretending to fish or fight, the women pretending to scold the men.

"You want me to show you what we learned last week?" Mel executed a little dance step, shuffling and clapping his hands up by his head.

"I'll pick it up," said Sydney. She scanned the room for someone else to talk to.

Mel looked her over, eyes moving up, down, up. He tried to take her hand, but she put it behind her back, out of his reach. "You ought to wear skirts like that all the time," he said. "You have nice hips. A really womanly body. So many women are ashamed of their bodies, but you seem to fit yours perfectly."

Sydney felt her face burning. Every week she tried to dodge and dive, so she wouldn't have to talk to him or stand beside him in the circles or be paired with him in the couple's dances. But he trailed her relentlessly. "I'm not really a woman," she said. "I'm only sixteen."

"Then you're a little woman. How's that?"

Sydney pointed in the direction of the bathroom. "Excuse me," she said. "Gotta go." She hid there until the music started then found a place in the circle where she wouldn't have to stand near Mel or look at him. She concentrated on learning the butcher's dance.

Afterward, Sydney sprinted to the coat rack, but Mel was right behind her, helping her into her coat, walking her out. Waiting for the traffic to clear, Sydney looked across the street at her car, which she had managed to parallel park in a small space in front of the grinder shop. "I don't need help crossing the street," she said.

"Can I treat you to a lemonade?" Mel asked. Sydney shook her head and stepped off the curb. Mel followed so closely that he grazed her heel, pulling her shoe partway off. "Maybe you're not thirsty," said Mel.

"I'm not."

At the car Sydney looked in her purse for her keys, and Mel stood right beside her. Then suddenly, a blur of nose and teeth as Mel's face swooped toward hers: he kissed her. He pulled back and gave a little smile. Sydney stared at him.

"I just wanted to do that," he said. "You're so beautiful."

Sydney unlocked the door and slid into the driver's seat.

"See you next week," he said.

Sydney nodded. She closed the door but didn't lock it, even though she wanted to. Mel stood on the sidewalk, waving.

"Asshole," said Sydney, as soon as he was no longer in sight. "Jerk." She turned onto a side street and parked the car under a no-parking sign. She felt greasy, cheated, furious. Mel's damp lips touching hers. God. She opened the door, leaned out, spit on the pavement. "Fucker," she said.

Oh, honey," Molly said, her voice full of sympathy, when Sydney called her. "He did that to me once."

"He did?"

"Once. I popped him in the eye. Did you hit him?"

"I was too surprised."

"Just a second," said Molly. "Tyler is throwing hot dogs, and Griffen is screaming." Sydney heard the clatter of the phone being dropped, then the various sounds of mayhem. She thought of how Molly had always talked of going to law school after college, but instead she got married and pregnant and pregnant again.

Sydney examined the postcard that had come from her parents. The writing was smeared and sloppy—hastily written—but they wished her well; they wished she was with them. Wherever they were. Sydney read the tiny print in the corner of the postcard: Gold Coast, Australia (Printed in Japan). Somewhere on its journey, the card had gotten folded in half. Several thin, white lines ran down the center of the postcard, neatly bisecting a palm tree.

What did it matter that her parents were gone? What difference did it make? When Frank came in her room last summer, her parents were in the next bedroom, ten feet away, snoring, useless.

"I swear," said Molly when she picked up the phone again. "The kid is in training to be a terrorist."

"Do you want me to baby-sit this weekend?" Sydney offered. "I could sleep over. You and Rick could stay out really late if you wanted to."

"That's so nice of you. But we're going to Rick's parents this weekend. A big Parker family reunion."

"Oh," said Sydney. "That's too bad."

"Tyler, what are you doing now?" Sydney heard her nephew whining in the background. "I better go," said Molly. "But listen, Sydney, if Mel tries it again, belt him. Make a scene."

"I'm not going anymore," said Sydney. "It's not worth it."

"Oh, honey," said Molly.

Sydney waited anxiously, all Friday, all Saturday, but Frank never came, never called. Two weekends gone, six to go. With any luck she wouldn't see him again until Christmas. Maybe he thought all his brotherly obligations were taken care of with that box of doughnuts, that one nice gesture.

On Sunday she called Carmen and Tammy and Sue, and they worked all afternoon on a new routine—practically finished it. They moved the coffee table and had plenty of room to march and kick and dance. Afterward they lolled on the floor, drinking root beer and eating Mystic Mints, having contests to see who could do the splits the longest.

Sydney told them about Mel kissing her.

"You should see this guy," said Carmen. "He's old and ugly. He's totally skigged."

Sue stretched her legs into Chinese splits then leaned forward until she was flat against the floor, her legs and trunk forming perfect right angles. "What if he was younger?" She spoke into the striped carpet. "Would you like him then?"

"He's bald!" yelled Carmen. "Get it? No hair."

"What if he was cute?" asked Tammy. "What if he was cute and he kissed you?"

"If it was my boyfriend, okay," said Sydney. "But I don't want random people to grab me and kiss me."

"It's just a question," said Tammy. "Don't get mad." She wandered around the living room, looking at everything, picking up dolls, books, doilies. She counted the portraits of Sydney's brothers and sisters. "Big family," she said. "Who's this? He's cute."

"My brother, Frank. He's not cute."

"He looks cute to me," said Tammy.

"You think everyone is cute," said Sue, her face pressed into the carpet.

Sydney stood at the front door, debating. Coat on, gloves on, keys out. Should she go? She thought of Mel talking to her, touching her, Mel's face right in her face, his pores, his nose hairs, Mel kissing her.

Finally she kicked the closed door, hurting her toes, which were enclosed in flimsy black Chinese slippers. She punched her father's big blue recliner; her hand sank dully into the cushion. Then she squatted down and lifted the chair from the bottom, her hands gripping bare, splintery wood. The chair tipped slowly, landed with a plump. "I can't go," she said. "Thank you very much." On the patch of carpet where the chair had been, she found a nickel and six pennies, a comb and an earring, dust and popcorn kernels. She took off her coat and gloves, picked up the larger items, vacuumed the rest.

Then on Thursday the washer broke. When Sydney got home from school, she carried a basket of dirty clothes to the basement and found gray water everywhere. She bailed and mopped, certain that she would be electrocuted. Her parents hadn't prepared her for anything like this happening; Sydney wasn't sure what to do. She figured she could get by for a while by just washing her underwear in the sink—

she had enough clothes for a week or two. When things got desperate, she could look up a laundromat in the phone book and drive there. She would buy little boxes of laundry soap from a machine and sit in a chair and read a magazine, the way people did in movies and in college. She would save her dimes and quarters in a jar.

$\mathcal{T}$he next night, Friday, Sydney was supposed to wait tables at Waid's, but she got sent home from the restaurant because business was so slow.

She went to her house and waited.

She waited, and then Frank arrived, lugging a duffel bag full of dirty laundry.

"It's broken," said Sydney.

Frank dropped the bulging bag in the middle of the living room and scowled. The string tie on the canvas bag came loose, and clothes spilled out. "Why didn't you call someone and get it fixed?"

"I don't know who to call."

"Just open a phone book."

"You call," said Sydney.

"You live here. I'm just baby-sitting." He flopped on the sofa, put his boots on her math book. Sydney yanked it away. "Whatcha watching?" he asked.

"Nothing," said Sydney. "Watch what you want." Reaching for the remote, Frank moved his hand in front of Sydney's face; for a second she could see nothing but the lines on his palm. For that instant she felt reckless. She wanted to bite his hand, make him bleed.

Frank settled into a sitcom. Sydney went into the kitchen and mixed cookie dough in a heavy glass bowl. She rolled the dough into tiny, perfect balls, lined them in straight rows on a cookie sheet. Then, sitting on the floor in front of the oven window, Sydney watched the balls spread into small, perfect circles. She breathed in the sweet smell of chocolate, listened to the bursts of sound-track laughter coming from the living room. She wondered if sound tracks ever fooled people into thinking a show was funny.

As soon as the first batch was laid out on paper towels, Frank materialized and started grabbing, throwing cookies into his mouth—a half dozen cookies in each of his big hands.

"Don't!" shouted Sydney.

"Why not?" said Frank, grabbing, chewing. "Are they poison?"

"They're for my lunches. I'm going to freeze them."

"Make some more."

Sydney banged a wooden chair hard against the kitchen table. The salt shaker fell over. "Don't come home anymore," she said. "I don't want you here."

"What are you so frizzed out about?" Frank stuck his finger into the bowl, scooped out a gob of dough.

Sydney pulled the bowl away, held it to her chest. "Get out," she commanded.

Later, she filled the bathtub with warm water and shampoo and submerged the clothes she would need for the next day: her drill team skirt and vest, her white turtleneck bodysuit, a pair of panties. She swished and scrubbed until the bubbles flattened, until the water turned dull and dirty.

After she hung up her clothes, Sydney lay in bed and reread a story in an old issue of *Seventeen*—her favorite story. The girl in the story was named Melody, and she classified kisses by color—meadow green, hot pink, crystal blue. Sydney fell asleep to the irregular sound of water dripping, dripping. She dreamed of Patrick Lefferson, of red-hot candy kisses, purple Popsicle kisses.

She woke feeling hands on her. Frank by her bed. Hands on her thighs, her breasts, between her legs. She turned and kicked, pretending to be asleep. He moved his hands away. Stood there, just stood there. Sydney choked back the vomit rising in her throat, but the awful taste stayed in her mouth. Tears burned in her eyes. In her mind, she counted, sixty seconds, sixty more; the seconds piled up, specks of nothing. What was he doing? Maybe he was touching himself, getting off just looking at her. Maybe he knew she was awake; maybe he was watching her tremble, watching her count. Maybe he was going to break all her bones, fold her up, and put her in a dresser drawer. He was strong from lifting weights, big, hard arms and hands. She could hear Nicole screaming in a field in Kansas, her body crumpled and abandoned and nothing but wheat for miles around.

If he raped her, she would drive to the police. Or call her parents. Or keep quiet.

She counted, counted, and then he left. Sydney heard him close the door, heard the scrape of wood on carpet.

She lay in her bed, shaking. From under her pillow she took a plastic baggie: Myrtle's ear, damp and smelly, coated with tissue fuzz. She had meant to shove it into Frank's face. He would be horrified or he would think she was crazy. Sydney didn't care which. But when the time came, Sydney's plan crumbled; her weapon was worthless, a moldy pig ear.

When she came downstairs the next morning, Frank was sitting at the kitchen table. He didn't look up, and Sydney didn't speak to him. She got her keys and her purse and drove to McDonald's, where she ate half an Egg McMuffin and drank a Coke. Sitting in the uncomfortable, molded-plastic chair, she wondered what would happen if she called the police. Frank would go to jail and her family would hate her. Her parents would have to stop going on trips; they would have to stay home and guard her. They would have to decide whether to believe Frank or whether to believe her. And what had he done?

Sydney bought a box of McDonaldland cookies and drove to

Molly's house. Her nephew, Tyler, was playing on the kitchen floor with a spoon and a beach ball. Sydney hoisted him, hugged him, kissed him. She gave him the cookies. "Do you love me?" she asked.

"Can you say it?" Molly coaxed him. "I love you, Aunt Sydney."

"I love you," said Tyler. He opened the box of cookies, tore past the cardboard and wax paper. He ate one, then began to cry. "I want french fries," he said. "French fries."

"Oh, boy," said Sydney. "Sorry."

"No, no," said Molly. "It was nice of you. He's being naughty."

"There's a basketball game tonight. We're performing at halftime. That's what I wanted to tell you." Sydney hoped she didn't sound desperate. Or she hoped she did. She hoped Molly would come to the game. "If you're bored . . ."

"Maybe I'll call Frank," said Molly.

Sydney nodded, gathered her things. "That's all," she said. "I just wanted to tell you."

Frank wasn't home when Sydney got there. She didn't see his duffel bag. Maybe he'd decided to drive back to KU and do his laundry there.

Sydney took a long, hot shower. She ate all the cookies she had baked the night before. She sat in the recliner and did the exercises in her French book, working three chapters ahead, checking the answer key frequently. For long stretches, she couldn't remember how to move, how to breathe.

At four o'clock she put on her drill team uniform—still slightly damp. But when she went to put on her socks, she couldn't find any clean ones. She dug a pair out of the hamper, dabbed at the dirty spots with a wet washcloth. She tied her shoes with double knots, then sat in the chair, glancing periodically at her watch until it was time to go.

The basketball team at her school was playing the basketball team from Patrick Lefferson's school. Maybe she could call him, thought

Sydney, ask if he would be at the game. Maybe she could tell him what had happened the night before. Whatever it was that had happened.

A bustle backstage, girls stretching out. They did high kicks in front of each other. "Does anything show?" they asked. Often during performances, boys would sit in the front rows of the bleachers and make rude comments. Red bloomers, blue bloomers, big and blousy like antique underwear. "Does anything show?" Sydney was always careful to shave pubic hairs that might slip past the elastic.

With two minutes still to go on the time clock, the girls lined up under the bleachers, rustling their pompons and waiting. Above their heads, hundreds of people sat and stood, and the rods and supports bucked and vibrated. The air smelled of hairspray, perfume, shoe polish. The floor was sticky with gum and spilled soda. Someone handed Sydney a jar of Vaseline. She dipped a finger into the goo, smeared a bit across her teeth to make her smile more slippery, to make it possible. Poise and smiles—those were what mattered. It wasn't uncommon for someone to botch steps during a performance or to blank out on part of a routine. If that happened, the girls had been trained to shake their pompons on the beat and smile, smile! Most of the time no one in the audience knew the difference.

The buzzer sounded for the half. The girls filed out, marched to their places, stood waiting for the music. Sydney stood straight and tried to sparkle. She looked up into the crowd—boys and girls, women and men, faces, eyes.

Not too far away she saw Patrick Lefferson sitting with a bunch of other boys she didn't know, boys from his new school. They all wore green sweatshirts and caps on their heads, and they leaned in close to talk, to jostle one another. Sydney saw that Patrick's shoulders had grown broad and strong; his neck was thick; his face was square. He was no one who could help her. He was just another boy, just a boy spitting tobacco juice into a big plastic cup.

Sydney counted eight beats, then started the kick add-on, placing her arms on the shoulders of the girls next to her for balance. Four kicks and then two more girls joined in. All together Sydney had to do thirty-two kicks, more than anyone else in her line. Her skirt flying up, her legs open. She saw Molly and Tyler sitting in the stands, sitting in their clean socks, a million miles from knowing. They were looking right at her, waving, smiling. Griffen was propped up in a car seat. Frank sat with them.

Her parents were half a world away, sitting under a palm tree. Her parents were a postcard.

Thirty-two kicks, but she kept a smile on her face as she had been trained to do. And one, and two, and three, and four. Her teeth were greasy with Vaseline. Her lips felt loose. They felt as if they were sliding off her face. Spray your hair, watch your weight. Jump kick, jump kick. Have fun, be classy. Jump kick, jump kick.

Nicole on the trampoline. Nicole in a ditch.

CHICKEN TRAIN

*O*n the sill above the sink, C.J.'s peach, nearly ripe, sat demurely.
C.J.'s wife, Ellen, stood nearby, washing lettuce, while C.J. himself sat
at the kitchen table, working a crossword and listening for sex. He
kept one ear tilted toward the basement, where his son and his son's
girlfriend had been holed up for an hour.

"One-oh-six across," said C.J. "Western eggs. Seven letters."

"No idea." Ellen's voice was dim and uninterested, half drowned
by the rush of tap water. C.J. wondered if she'd even heard him. He
studied her from behind, trying to predict the quick movements of
her elbows as they poked the air. Ellen's brown hair hung to her
shoulders, limp and uninspired. Her shorts pulled tight across her rear
end; her legs were pale and soft. C.J. knew that sometimes she wore
a long shirt and left her pants unfastened, giving herself room to
breathe. When they met in high school, so many years before, Ellen
had been tiny, but C.J. didn't hold tightly to that version of her. In
fact, he couldn't hold on to that version at all. Over the years, her figure

had changed so gradually that he usually couldn't remember her looking any different from the way she looked at the present moment. Only sometimes—unexpectedly—his memory would flash an image, bright and dizzying, like a slide shown out of sequence: Ellen at sixteen in a tight, pink sweater; Ellen at the far end of the church aisle, looking small yet imposing in her white wedding dress.

He watched as she grasped a mass of wet lettuce, moved her hand slowly up, then quickly down, the leaves mimicking the arc and crack of a whip. Several drops landed on the crossword in egg-shaped ovals. "Scrambled," said C.J., counting letters on his fingers.

"Huevos rancheros," Ellen suggested.

"Doesn't fit." C.J. leaned forward on his elbows and pressed his head with his hands. He'd seen very old men adjusting their brains in this way, trying to force out one last thought. At the window a hot summer breeze pushed past the kitchen curtains—a moment later the aroma of the peach wafted into C.J.'s consciousness.

He stood and moved toward the sink. Reaching past Ellen's shoulder, he lifted the peach from the windowsill.

"Mmm," she said softly, leaning back.

C.J. stepped away from her and with both hands gently cupped the peach. He closed his eyes and inhaled, felt the brush of fuzz against his lips—velvet stiffness, tender bristles. He touched the peach to his teeth—saliva gathered in his mouth, and he held to the moment of waiting, to the thought of warm, sweet juice. He was reminded of the feelings he'd had when he was seventeen, eighteen, when he and Ellen had spent so many evenings swaying on the brink of making love, holding themselves at the moment just before, the time of pure anticipation. Raging anticipation. The dark, tense, hazy moments before they closed zippers and composed themselves and slipped into their parents' houses.

Yet it wasn't quite the same, this peach held to his lips—this was calmer, sweeter, more assured. And in this moment he sensed, he believed, that all things in the world were his for the taking. He lowered the peach. "Almost," he said. "Almost ready."

"The Almighty Peach." Ellen snapped her wrist, sprinkling C.J.'s shirt, his glasses. "I hate to think what would happen if somebody ate it. You'd either cry or kill them."

C.J.'s thin shoulders folded in, and he shielded the peach in the semicircle his body had formed. "No one eats this peach," he declared. "No one. Never." In a drawer jammed with warranties and twist ties, he found an index card and a felt-tip pen. He printed a note in square blue letters: PLEASE—DO NOT EAT THIS PEACH. He propped this warning against the peach and returned to his place at the table. Ellen hauled a jar of sauerkraut out of the refrigerator, unscrewed the top, sniffed.

"We'll have Reubens," she announced.

"Fine."

"Unless you want eggs."

"No," said C.J. "Whatever. One-forty-three across. Rowdydow." He pressed his head. Rowdydow. Was that anything like a roustabout? What was a roustabout anyway?

He craned his neck toward the basement stairs and listened, listened past the music that drifted up. Was that the snap of an elastic waistband? A giggle? A moan? He folded the magazine, slapped it down onto the table. He stood again, held his ear against the Sierra Club calendar that was thumbtacked to the door, and listened through the glossy, purple mountains. "If they were hamsters," he whispered, "we'd buy them separate cages."

"Oh, C.J.," said Ellen. "You're so romantic." She unwrapped a package of corned beef and separated the slices. The spicy, meaty smell that filled the room reminded C.J. of dead things, of festering sores.

"Sixteen-year-olds do not belong in bedrooms," he said.

"Angie is seventeen. She just had her birthday."

C.J. snorted. "Oh, gee. Seventeen." He could imagine them squeezed together on Charlie's twin bed—naked and giggling—their underwear hanging off the corners of the stereo speakers.

"They're not going to do anything when we're ten feet away."

"That's right." C.J. flung open the door. "They're not." He descended noisily, his shoes scraping on the concrete stairs. He felt his body heating up, sweat spreading across his forehead. As a high school teacher, he was used to teenagers, but it was one thing to guide them through *Lord of the Flies,* and another thing entirely to live with them. In the last week, for instance, he'd seen his daughter, Ceci, making out in the driveway twice—a different boy and a different car on each occasion.

"If it bothers you, don't watch," she said when he brought it up as a topic of conversation.

C.J. gave one last rap at the bottom of the stairs. Entering the small, gray room, he found Charlie and Angie cuddling in an old armchair, a huge, gold velvet monstrosity; they lifted their heads and looked over the back of the chair at him. Charlie raised his hand lazily in greeting.

"Isn't this nice." C.J. sat on the bed, bounced a few times. "Kiss, kiss, kiss."

"It's not bad." Charlie smiled, drew Angie closer. "I was telling Angie about the chicken," he said.

"Beer and butter," said C.J. "Nothing better."

"You can't stop eating," said Charlie. "It's so good."

"It sounds good," said Angie.

The gold chair faced the stereo, and they all watched the records go round and round. C.J. lay back, dangling his shoes off the edge of the bed; he stretched and settled himself, ran his fingers along the surface of the bedspread, the rough polyester ribs. He wondered if Charlie and Angie really did make love in this bed. From his prone position, he could see Charlie stroking Angie's arm, her hand, her fingers. Though the two looked drowsy and peaceful, C.J. could guess what they were feeling—beneath the skin their bodies were singing. He remembered the sensation from when he was younger, back when kissing Ellen made him feverish, when it seemed he spent most of each day with his body tingling, aching, alive.

Now, lying on Charlie's narrow bed, C.J. tried to gather some of his son's energy into himself, but nothing happened; nothing changed.

Music oozed from the speakers, and Charlie sang along softly.

"Oh," cooed C.J. " 'Two cats in the yard.' Isn't that sweet?"

"It's something to shoot for," said Charlie.

C.J. propped himself on his elbows. "How about you, Angie? You think this is how it is? Two cats, a vase? You think so?"

"I never said it was my philosophy of life. It's just a song."

C.J. watched Angie's face turn red. She'd been his student as a freshman, and even in a generous state of mind he had trouble understanding what Charlie saw in her. Her pert little ponytail? Her cheerleader legs? "You must like it," he said, "or you wouldn't be listening to it."

"I do like it," said Angie.

C.J. suppressed his immediate reaction, which was to mimic Angie's words back at her. He did that in class sometimes; it was a tactic that always got a big laugh and almost always left him feeling ashamed.

Charlie used his foot to turn the chair toward C.J. The ancient swivelling mechanism squeaked and groaned. "Is there something you want to say to us? Are you down here for some reason?"

"Gosh, no," C.J. said breezily. "I'm just visiting." He lay back on the bed and, bringing his leg close to his face, casually scratched his bare knee. "Just trying to delay the inevitable."

"We don't need to be chaperoned," said Charlie, "if that's what you're doing." He shifted, repositioning Angie on his lap. "We're not fucking now, and we don't have any plans for fucking tonight."

C.J. was off the bed in an instant, moving toward Charlie. He thought for a second of grabbing a handful of his son's hair, pulling the way he'd pull against the most tenacious dandelion. Instead he placed his hand flat on Charlie's head and pushed down hard. Charlie sat passively, a blank expression on his face; his arms protruded from his green and yellow tank top, and he gripped the armrests of the golden chair.

"Fuck all you want," said C.J. "Flunk out of high school, have three kids—have six kids. Be my guest." C.J. lifted his hand, made a sweeping gesture of invitation. "You think it's two cats in the yard? I'll tell you where you'd be if you got married now. You'd be living in some basement apartment, using soup cans for dishes."

Charlie smiled slightly. "I live in the basement now."

"Well, you'd better watch your step because it's kissy, kissy, and the next thing you know, it's diapers and baby shit, and your life is shot to hell."

"Dad." Charlie stared straight into C.J.'s eyes. "Let me steer you back to reality here. We're sitting in a chair, listening to music. We're not flunking out of school."

Angie said nothing.

Ellen called from upstairs, cheery and oblivious. "The Reubens are ready."

"Well," said C.J. slapping his hands on his bare thighs. "Let's eat." His legs stung from the impact, but he wanted to hit himself again. He clapped his hands together instead.

"There's plenty, Angie, if you want to stay," Ellen said.

C.J. watched as Charlie and Angie hoisted themselves out of the chair. Angie's shirt was crooked, her ponytail unraveling. A blurred memory passed through C.J.'s mind as he looked at her, a long-ago image of Ellen—young and sleepy and excited, lipstick smeared here and there across her face.

Now Charlie was standing barefoot on the concrete floor. He was tall, and he pulled himself taller. "Is it okay with you if I kiss Angie good-bye?" he asked, politely, aggressively, his face pinched now, and ugly. "Do I have your permission?"

C.J. folded his arms and planted himself in front of them. "Be my guest."

Charlie swooped down sloppily, dramatically, but Angie pushed away before the intended kiss was half finished. She went upstairs without speaking to either of them. At the kitchen, she opened the door and said something to Ellen.

"You're coming to the party, aren't you, Angie?" C.J. called. "I'm making chicken." The screen door slammed, and then a car door opened and closed. C.J. looked at Charlie. "Maybe she didn't hear me. I hope she comes."

Charlie stared at him, and C.J. stared back, stared so long that Charlie began to blend into the shadows and angles of the basement. The room seemed like a submarine, dark and enclosed and moving slowly forward. C.J. knew he should apologize. When he told Ellen what had happened, she would insist upon it.

With a series of clicks, the needle arm on the record player lifted and shifted and then dropped into its holder. The light on the stereo went out, and the room was still. C.J. smiled.

"What are you laughing at?" Charlie asked, scowling.

"You already live in the basement," said C.J., and he did laugh then. He laughed so hard he had to sit down on the bed. He laughed until Charlie joined in.

Charlie sat sideways in the chair, his legs hanging over one plush, upholstered arm. "You're such an asshole," he said.

"Yep."

Ellen's head reappeared. "I'm starting without you," she said.

$\mathcal{T}$he next day, the day of the party, was hot and sticky. The newspaper mentioned the possibility of thunderstorms and the certainty of heat. C.J. and Ellen stood in the living room, hashing out the details: parking arrangements, folding chairs, picnic tables.

"Let me just tell you where I stand," said Ellen. She had wrapped a red bandanna around her head, a style she adopted only once or twice a year, in times of frenzied cleaning. "I don't want people coming inside at all. *At all.* Everyone muddy and sweaty. Little kids touching the walls. You know how it gets."

"People have to use the bathrooms," said C.J.

"Well, I don't want anyone using the half bath, and I want plastic on the floor and plastic on my sofa. Anywhere anyone might walk or touch or sit."

From nineteen years of marriage, C.J. knew that the best cure for Ellen's irritability was for him to leave the house. Soothing words or compromises or comedy—especially comedy—would just make her more furious. He didn't leave, though. "Here's what we'll do," he said. "We'll cover the whole house in plastic, and we'll call it art. We'll invite everyone to come in and look at it."

"No one is coming in the house!"

"Ellen, okay, listen. We won't have the party. We'll call everyone and tell them we're sick. We threw up all night. The house smells terrible."

"No!" shouted Ellen. "We're not calling anyone!"

"Fine," said C.J. "Fine." He left her pacing the living room and set out for supplies. In the meantime, Ellen could take a bath, hide the toilet paper, whatever might help her calm down. There would be one more crisis—maybe two—and then the party would take off; it would take over, and everything would be fine. Ellen would relax. She would eat and laugh and enjoy herself. And when everyone left, late, late in the night, the two of them, Ellen and C.J., would lie in bed and talk of the music and the food and the people, of all that had happened and all that had been said.

C.J. pulled the car out of the garage. Rolling along the drive, he glanced at his lap, double-checked his seat belt. When he looked up a moment later, he saw a woman, a girl—Pam Galvin—heading toward the house. C.J. stuck his head out the car window and called to her—"Pammie!"

Hopping out of the car, he approached her, ready to hug her or rumple her hair—some rough affection for a neighbor kid who had moved away. But when he stood in front of her, C.J. knew that he couldn't do either of those things. Since the last time he'd seen her— just a few months before—Pam's little girl body had changed. It had matured into something amazing, into hips and breasts and legs, slim and full and adorable.

She was beautiful, a clear blue sky with irises blooming. She was twelve, thirteen.

Sternly, silently, C.J. spoke to himself: There are laws, he said. You're forty-one years old.

Pam wore bright yellow shorts and a white T-shirt that said Roeland Park Swimming. Her hair was brown and gold and red—C.J. tried to classify it and couldn't. He thought of Ellen in the house, her hair tied up in a rag.

The name tumbled out of his mouth again. "Pammie." His voice sounded hollow and strange. He couldn't remember—was that what everyone called her, or was it only him? Had he ever called her Pammie before? Face to face with this Pam, C.J. could hardly remember the other, younger one.

Pam held out an orange extension cord. "My dad said you wanted this."

"Great!" C.J. flung his arms wide, clasped his hands, opened wide again. Now he was smiling; he couldn't stop smiling. "Terrific!" He took the cord from her and held it to his chest.

Pam put her hands behind her back. She smiled. "It's almost time for the chicken train."

C.J. forced his face into a frown. "This year I want everyone to stay out of the tomato plants. Out of the garden. Off-limits absolutely. You started that last year, didn't you?" C.J. pointed at her in mock accusation, teasing. "You were the ringleader."

"I was not," protested Pam. She pushed him, a touch as soft as cotton. C.J. pretended to stagger backward. "You be quiet."

"Wait a minute." C.J. grasped his chin in one hand and pretended to think. "Maybe it was me." He motioned her around the corner of the house. "Come in," he said. "Please come in." He wanted to put his hand on her back and guide her into the house, show her off to Ellen.

"My mom's in the car."

"Your mom's in the car." Now C.J. looked toward the street. Pam's mother, Marjo, lifted one hand from the steering wheel and smiled. She motioned Pam to get back in the car.

"Thank you," C.J. said to Pam. He wanted to say, "You're beautiful," but he waited a second too long, and then it was too late, a hundred years beyond spontaneity. "Bye-bye," he said.

Standing in the driveway, holding tight to Pam's extension cord, C.J. watched her walk away. He breathed in the smells of heat and summer—the zinnias in the flower bed, the roses that edged the lawn, the tar that bubbled beneath his feet.

*T*he second crisis was under way when C.J. got home. Ceci opened his car door and launched into her side of the story: "I wouldn't mind that Mom tries on my clothes if she would just hang them up again. But no—everything is on the floor like a big tornado."

"Don't yell." C.J. put a finger to his lips in warning.

"Every pair of pants—she takes them out of the closet, and she doesn't even want to wear them. She just wants to feel bad that they don't fit."

C.J. watched Ceci's mouth move, watched her bright red lips form circles and lines and pinched little puckers. He tried to make sense of what she was telling him.

"I'll talk to her," he said and drifted toward the house in a dreamy haze, the lingering effect of his encounter with Pam. He felt benevolent, but unconnected; willing to serve as peacemaker, yet utterly uninterested in the outcome.

Inside, Ellen was dusting with a tattered pair of boy's underpants, moving randomly from room to room, flicking her cloth here and there. She had changed into a shirt with matching shorts, an outfit C.J. had given her as a birthday present. Her hair was neatly arranged, the bangs curled and fluffed.

C.J. stood in the doorway that connected the living room and the kitchen and watched her. He thought of the night he first met Ellen— a high school party in somebody's basement. Ellen had worn bright red pants, and in C.J.'s memory she never stopped moving, never stopped laughing. C.J. had leaned up against a paneled wall and watched her dance. By the end of the night, he'd met her, danced with her, fallen in love.

Now C.J. coughed to clear his throat. "You look nice," he said.

Ellen bent down and swiped her rag along the dustboard. "You have good taste."

He thought of Pam's shiny hair, her smile, the muted pink of her fingernails. He wasn't sure what to say next. Then he pictured Ceci circling the house, muttering to herself, and that image drove him forward. "Look," said C.J. "Ceci was saying—"

Ellen straightened. "Don't start on me."

"Don't worry about it." C.J. spoke in a quiet voice, almost a monotone, the voice he would use on a kitten or a baby. "Of course Ceci's clothes don't fit you. She's fifteen. You think what she wears now is going to fit *her* when she's your age? Don't worry. Everything comes around."

"Sure," said Ellen. "And when Ceci's forty-two, I'll probably weigh three hundred pounds." She moved into the kitchen and dusted the phone.

C.J. followed close behind, leaned against the doorframe. He watched her hand move along the receiver, watched her rub at the mouthpiece. He wanted to restrain her, hold her arms. Do something else, he wanted to say. Do something better. "Or else you'll be dead," he said.

Ellen stood still, and the phone cord knocked against the wall— once, twice. She turned to look at him. "That's a nice thought," she said, and laughed.

"Just relax," said C.J. He moved his hand across the back of her hair, smoothing, stroking, and he thought of where he'd be when Ceci was forty-two, when Ellen was three hundred pounds—he'd be far, far away from here. He'd be in Vermont, living on an apple farm with Pam.

"I am relaxed. I'm relaxed. I . . . am . . . relaxed." She spent half a minute at the sink, polishing the spigot, then worked her way up to the windowsill. She read C.J.'s sign out loud: " 'Please—do not eat this peach.' " Irritation stained her voice. "How long am I going to have to look at this damn thing? People are going to think we're fools."

"Who's going to see it? I thought you said no one could come in the house."

"Well, we can't very well invite guests over and ask them to pee in the yard, can we?" Ellen worked her rag over a pane of glass, pressing so hard her fingertips turned white. "If they want to come in, we'll have to let them."

"I agree," said C.J. quietly. "I agree." He turned the sign over and laid it flat on the sill beside the peach. "Okay?"

The fragrance was mouthwatering—alluring. The skin was red and pink and orange, vividly hued and silky to the touch. Part of C.J. wanted to eat the peach now. Part of him wanted to leave it on the sill forever.

"Why don't you just eat the thing and get it over with?" Ellen moved her finger toward the peach, as if she intended to jab a hole in it. "Look how soft it is."

"Don't!" C.J. put his hands over the peach the way a fourth-grader guards his spelling test. "Don't touch it."

For a moment, Ellen let the dust cloth dangle idly at her side; her voice was mild, amused. "Just eat it."

𝒯he backyard was bright with streamers and balloons and pink petunias in wooden boxes. Along the fence on the left side of the yard, C.J. had rigged up a fountain that trickled greenish water over a concrete statue of St. Francis of Assisi. A basketball hoop sagged from above the doorway of the garage, and beyond, out of view, lay C.J.'s garden, the place he spent most days in summer.

Guests started drifting in by late afternoon, early evening. They exchanged hugs and handshakes and piled the tables with food. Ellen loosened the foil on the various dishes and peeked at the offerings— beans and salads and deviled eggs, brownies and cookies and cakes. C.J. stood beside the grill, dodging smoke as best he could, tinkering with the fire and watching the guests, watching for new arrivals. For now he was rooted in his spot, but once the chicken was ready, he could do whatever he wanted, wander and mingle and talk to whomever he pleased. And then later, much later, when it was good and dark, when everyone was drunk or on the way to being drunk, he would lead the chicken train. They would dance through the yard and shout and sing, and C.J. would weave strings of people into bouncing, bobbing, laughing patterns, under, over, around and around.

When Pam arrived with her parents, C.J. was inside, pulling the plastic wrap off Styrofoam trays of chicken. By the time he got back outside, the family had dispersed. Marjo was busying about the food table, and Pam's father, Mitch, had established himself in the horseshoe game. Pam stood in the driveway, apart from the crowd, talking to Charlie, and C.J. held his plate of pale meat and watched them. He scanned the crowd for Angie. If he found her, he'd point at Charlie, tell her to keep an eye on him. He'd say, "If you love him, you've got to watch him."

"Hey, dreamboat." Ellen bumped C.J.'s arm. "You'd better check that chicken." Assessing the smoke and flames in a glance, he dashed to the grill, began plucking pieces of chicken off the rack and piling them on a plate. Another five or ten seconds and his barbecue reputation would have been shot. Balancing the loaded platter, C.J. nudged his way through the crowd, offering thighs and legs. Ellen followed behind with napkins and little paper plates.

"C.J. thinks everyone is as barbaric as he is," she said, laughing, digging a finger into his side as if to tickle him, although she knew full well he wasn't ticklish.

He looked for Pam, but she had disappeared; Charlie, too. But once C.J. returned to his post at the grill, Charlie sidled up, grabbed a drumstick, took a bite. "Did you see Pam?" he asked, his mouth slick with grease. "Did you see the squirt?"

"What about her?" C.J. dipped his basting brush into his special sauce. He smeared a thigh.

Charlie shook his head, his eyes darting over to where Angie sat at a folding table under an awning. "My God," he said. "I hope I'm never as old as you are." He traced the outline of an impossible hourglass shape with his hands. "She's the most beautiful thing I've ever seen. She could be in a calendar." At the food table, Pam ate a brownie off a napkin. C.J. and Charlie stood transfixed, watching her lick chocolate off her fingers. "Just think," said Charlie. "I used to be mean to her."

C.J. shook his head to break his gaze. "She's eleven years old," he said. "She's a child. You're too old for her."

"She's not a child. She's thirteen—that was old enough for Jerry Lee. Old enough for Elvis. Besides," said Charlie, puffing himself up, "I'm only sixteen."

C.J. made a small incision into a piece of meat and examined the color. Pinkish. He'd give it another minute. "I thought you were in love."

"I am," said Charlie. "I am in love."

The next time C.J. raised his head from the fire, Charlie was swinging Pam through the air, turning her in circles as if she were a five-year-old, and Pam was batting him on the head and laughing.

A fleeting sunset, then steadily increasing dark. Near a circle of lawn chairs, the soft, purple glow of a bug zapper—some guest's contribution to the party. C.J. felt the hairs on his neck rise and tremble with each macabre crackle, each tiny execution.

In years past, C.J. and Ellen had tried to develop themes for the annual August party, decorating with Greek columns, Chinese lanterns, palm fronds. But more recently, they just relaxed and let the party fuel itself, on food and beer, darkness and adrenaline. Somehow everything got taken care of. When the ice ran out, someone would drive to the store and get more. When the call went up for sparklers, someone would pass them around, and for a few minutes the backyard would be wild with frenetic, fuzzy light.

C.J. wandered through the yard, free, finally. Charlie was at the grill now, tending to a final batch of chicken—necks and backs, bony pieces that Ellen didn't want to see wasted. Angie sat in a lawn chair nearby, drinking a soda and looking bored. Served her right, thought C.J. He felt bored every time she walked in a room, every time she opened her mouth.

C.J. felt fingers on his arm—a woman's fingers. Expecting Ellen, he turned his head to see Pam standing beside him, still touching him. Under her warm fingers, his skin felt damp and electric. "C.J.," she said, "do you have a basketball?"

In the garage, he dug through a box that held assorted, poorly cared-for sporting equipment: croquet mallets, roller skates, a foam football. He pulled out a crushed badminton racquet. "How about this?"

Pam laughed. "I would hardly call that a basketball."

Reaching deep into a corner of the box, C.J. leaned toward Pam until the hairs on his leg almost touched her. Among the smells of gas and oil, he smelled Pam, clean and floral, with a touch of chocolate, a hint of gingersnap. C.J. kept his head down in the box, pretending to search—pretending, because he had seen the ball a moment before, half-hidden by a rake, in a far corner of the garage. His mind sparked with disorderly fragments, memories of similar moments at other parties, in kitchens and corridors with women besides Ellen, times when he had been pulled along by blood or tides or perfume. Those times, his body had seemed to exist outside of his life. Those times, things had come along to kill the mood: a toilet had flushed, an ice maker had tumbled out a load of ice cubes, a clock had struck midnight, twelve slow gongs vibrating the air. Nothing ever happened; nothing had ever happened. There was only Ellen, always Ellen, only Ellen. Bedroom slippers and worn flannel pajamas. C.J. and Ellen having plain, tame sex, Friday-night, Sunday-morning sex. Sometimes they kept their socks on.

C.J. straightened, walked to the corner, picked up the ball.

"Do you want to play horse?" asked Pam. "If you miss a shot, you get a letter."

"I'll play horse," he said. "But I won't play *horse.*"

"What?"

"Let's play rowdydow instead."

Pam blinked. "How many letters?"

"R-O-W-D-Y-D-O-W. Eight."

"What is it? I mean, what is a rowdydow?"

"Do you know what a roustabout is?" asked C.J.

She shook her head.

"Neither do I." He bounced the ball to Pam; she caught it, then bounced it back.

"You go first," she said.

Pam took her shots from as far back as possible. She held her arms straight over her head, and when she threw the ball, her legs moved up while her arms moved down, her body folding up like a jackknife. She looked more like a modern dancer than a basketball player. The air escaped her lungs in a grunt, *huhhh.* The ball headed for the basket in a straight line, no arc, but to C.J.'s amazement, went in as often as not. She said "Shoot!" when she missed, crowed "Hah!" when the ball rattled in. When she shot, when she dribbled, when she raced after the ball, C.J. felt the eyes of the party following her, admiring her.

"R-O-W," said Pam.

"Okay." C.J. positioned himself, shuffling his feet until he felt properly connected with the asphalt. He outlined the requirements of his next shot. "Trick shot. You have to hit the roof—the edge there—and then bounce it in."

"That's impossible."

"No, it's not. I saw Ceci do it once. And now I shall demonstrate." C.J. aimed and released, and the ball sailed above the peak of the garage, clattered across the roof, and disappeared into the garden. He looked at Pam, and she burst into laughter. He stood in the circle of bright white cast by the garage light; a warm confidence crept through his body. "Rats," he said. "Let's get it."

They stepped through the narrow passage between the garage and the fence into the garden, into the strong, unlovely smell of marigolds.

"This is impossible," said Pam as they trudged through the rows. When she reached the near end of a row, she plumped down on the ground with her back against the garage. "I give up. You can find it in the morning. You're the one who threw it back here."

C.J. sat beside her. Pam's legs were folded into a cross-legged position, with her knees jutting upward. In the light of the moon, in the random bits of light from the party, C.J. thought he saw the glimmer of downy, pale hair on her legs. He wanted to smooth his hand along her leg, feel the rough, soft hair. Instead he clasped his hands together and dropped them onto the ground in front of him. In the background, he heard the thud of a horseshoe hitting the ground, and then a voice saying, "Give it up."

"If you could have been here when the irises were blooming," said C.J. "This whole part—irises, all colors."

"C.J.!" The shout rose above the buzz of the party, a voice he didn't recognize. "C.J.!"

"The best part," he said quietly, "is that they smell like whatever color they are. I mean the purple ones smell like grape, and the red ones smell like cherries." In the springtime, when the irises were blooming, C.J. spent afternoons wandering from flower to flower, breathing in the delightful smells. "You're wasting your life," Ellen would say. She would try to coax him to "do something"—hammer in a nail or go with her to the mall to buy a pair of socks. "I have to stay here," C.J. would answer. "When they're gone, they're gone forever." And sometimes then she would join him, walk in the sun in the muddy garden and smell the irises.

"What do the black ones smell like?" asked Pam.

"Like licorice," said C.J. "What else?"

"Really?" Pam squinted skeptically. "I don't believe you."

"Next year," said C.J., "you come over and I'll show you."

But the truth was unavoidable: he didn't want next year to come. Next year she would be older, harder, different. By then she would have a big, burly boyfriend who would make her cry, make her sour and mistrustful.

C.J. stood abruptly, wobbling a bit as the blood found its way to his head. "Stay here," he said. "Stay." He pushed down firmly on her shoulders as if to root her in the dirt. He ran to the end of the garage, then looked back.

She waved. "I'm right here."

He passed the crowd on the patio and ran inside. The light in the kitchen made his eyes blink and water. The table was littered with plastic cups—lost and abandoned, half-empty and half-full. The room smelled of bodies and cigarettes and peaches. Ceci was backed up against the refrigerator, kissing a boy whom C.J. could not identify— probably even Ceci didn't know who he was. Turning her head slowly, she looked at C.J. with eyes that were dreamy and glazed. Her lips were soft, full, almost purple. "Oh," she said. She looked at the boy, looked at C.J., then sank into another kiss.

C.J. stood for a moment, breathing in, breathing out. He was poised like a sprinter, one foot forward, one foot back. He could scream; he could scold; he could pull her away. He could hold out both his arms and try to stop the momentum, but he knew the gesture would be useless, foolish—he'd merely be flapping his arms.

Without a word, C.J. plucked the peach off the sill, grabbed a knife and a napkin, and banged his way through the kitchen door.

On the patio, a hand held out a tray of cupcakes and offered him one. "Not now," said C.J. "Later." Then he was back in the garden, among the thick, steamy smells.

He hunkered down in front of Pam and made the presentation. "For you," he said.

Her legs stretched out in front of her now; her back was flat against the garage. Her cheap canvas sneakers stuck out of the ground like jaunty flowers, like tulips. "Go ahead," said C.J. "It's for you." He had a picture in his mind of how she would look, juice dripping, her chin wet and shiny in the darkness. She would turn to him, laughing, and offer him a bite.

Pam held the peach in her hand as if trying to decide its weight, or its value. C.J.'s mouth was as dry and stiff as a cardboard box; he cleared his throat. He wanted to say something, but he didn't know what.

Pam wrinkled her nose, then C.J. did the same. The taint of cigarette smoke had mixed into the warm night air. Turning his head, C.J. saw Ellen at the corner of the garage, the red bud of a glowing cigarette in her hand. She only smoked at parties, at the tail end of parties.

She said, "What are you two doing?"

"We're appreciating the peach," said C.J.

"Your fucking peach." She came up behind C.J., loomed over him, bumped her knees into his back. His balance was precarious, and he tipped forward onto his knees. Tiny black flecks floated past his face, the dead ashes from her cigarette. "Come here," she said to C.J., lifting him, propelling him. They moved a few steps away from Pam, squeezed in between two rows of corn. A leaf brushed C.J.'s arm, and he jumped. "Leave her alone," said Ellen.

"I'm not doing anything."

"That's good. Because you'll go straight to jail, and you'll stay there forever."

"I'm not doing anything," he said. "I wouldn't." He turned away, walked back to where Pam was sitting. Ellen followed, the toes of her shoes clipping the heels of his.

Pam looked up at him. "Should I eat it?" she asked.

"Go ahead," said C.J. "It's for you."

"Aren't you lucky?" said Ellen. "You're a lucky little girl."

C.J. watched Pam handle the peach, waited for her to bite it. Instead, she took hold of the knife and began peeling awkwardly. C.J. watched as chunks of his peach fell to the ground. "I don't like the fuzz," she explained.

"Of course not," said C.J. "No one does. Peel away."

Ellen stood directly behind him, breathing on his neck, murmuring into his ear, "Twelve years old. Twelve years old."

"Thirteen," said C.J.

Pam cut a piece and passed it to C.J. on the blade of the knife. "You try it." She gave another slice to Ellen.

He chewed his bit of peach, and the flavors and sensations bloomed inside him, filled his mouth, his mind—bright as sunshine, sweet as honey, sour, spicy, mellow, wet.

"Not bad," said Ellen.

"Yum," breathed Pam, and C.J. smiled in the darkness. Pam sliced and ate, dripping, gobbling, beautiful and sticky. When she finished, she threw the pit into the tangle of cornstalks and said, "Grow!"

And then it was finished—his amazing peach, his brief delight.

From the other side of the garage, a shout went up, a chorus of voices—"C.J.! C.J.!"—and the notes of "Chicken Train" filtered through the din.

"Oh!" cried Pam, leaping to her feet. "Listen!"

When they reached the paved expanse of driveway, the chain had already formed, with Charlie at the lead. C.J. looked for Angie, but he couldn't find her among the mob.

Passing by, Charlie raised his hand, and C.J. met it in a high five, a resounding clap. "Get on!" shouted Charlie. "Come on!" He made a long, loud noise like a train whistle—"Whooo-whooo!"—and with one arm, lassoed Pam. He held her hand as he danced and gyrated; he pulled her along, and she giggled and screamed.

C.J. looked around and above at the shiny, blue-black night. He was surrounded by the twang of the instruments, by his neighbors and friends all flapping their arms in crazy poultry imitations. *"Running all day, running all night, can't get on, can't get off"*—he closed his eyes, and Pam danced behind his eyelids. When he opened them, she was everywhere, looking sometimes like a woman, sometimes like a child. C.J. could jump in front of her, jump behind her, try to grab her, try to hold her, but he didn't; he wouldn't.

Grabbing for Charlie's waistband, C.J. joined the dance. Ellen wedged in behind and wrapped her arms around C.J.'s waist, and C.J. got the feeling that she wanted to be there, that she wasn't just holding him to keep him from going someplace else. He reached back and grasped her hand, pressed it tightly to his hip. And they held each other that way—publicly, secretly—skin and cells and perspiration. He felt the hard lumps of knuckle, the thin, fine bones, Ellen's hand; he felt the joyous thump of his heartbeat, the blood hot and quick in his veins. As they snaked around the yard, as they stepped and hopped and stumbled, C.J. felt the party distill down to its elements—down to sweat and dirt and spinning circles with arms full of sparklers and whoops and hollers and dark corners and tongues against tongues and bodies against bodies and no one quite remembering what belongs to whom.

And when everyone had gone home, the two of them, C.J. and Ellen, would sit up in bed and talk of all that had happened, of all that had been said.

MISSY

*T*his isn't one of those jobs where you have to be busy all the time, polishing brass knobs and marrying bottles of ketchup. That was my last job, two dollars an hour and a three-page list of side work: mop out the bathrooms, refill the salt. Here, I don't have to do anything. I could slump against the counter for an hour, and no one would mind. But I'm restocking, nonetheless.

Carrie's out front squeezing jellybeans—releasing the essential oils, she says. At Madeline's we're allowed to eat as much as we want, but smelling is as far as Carrie goes.

Another thing: she has a boyfriend, but she doesn't kiss him, doesn't kiss anyone. "Too messy," she says. "Too involved." I kept quiet when she told me this, wondered if she could look at me and guess the things I do with my boyfriend, Richie. If Mrs. Spallo, my last year's religion teacher, knew about the no-kissing policy, she would invite Carrie to give a speech to the sophomores, the way she had the guidance counselor come to class and tell us about the mucus method of birth control. The class was called religion, but it was really sex education; I spent the whole semester staring at a poster that said, Not to Decide Is to Decide. To have sex or not to have sex, that is the question.

I'll tell you this: I'm still a virgin, but that's all I'm going to say.

The storeroom at Madeline's is bright and narrow, and the shelves are stacked with hundreds of white boxes, all of them bearing cryptic markings in black ink: Ch. Or. P., Pec. Trk., Sr. Blls. When I come in here, I feel hot, even though the temperature is normal—below normal, in fact, to keep the chocolate from drooping, from sliding off and exposing cherries and pretzels and pale cream centers. I'm surrounded by boxes, and sweat trickles from my armpits. People say thieves have itchy fingers, but it's worse than that for me—I'm itchy everywhere.

When I'm still at home, as I'm leaving for work, my family tells me what to bring. They stand in the doorway and yell; they come out to the car and beg. Chocolate peanuts, they say. Gummy bears. And turtles, please, turtles.

I'm going to have to quit this job.

Reaching, I pull down a box marked Al. Bar. (Wh.)—white almond bark. Inside, under puffs of plastic wrapping, the slabs lean up against one another like lumpy dominos. I pinch off a bit of bark and eat it. Sweet, creamy, nutty—it tastes all right, but how can chocolate be white? White chocolate makes no sense.

Out front again, kneeling behind the counter, I try to make Carrie laugh by gazing at the ceiling and singing "Ave Maria." When she gives a little smile, the corners of her mouth just barely turning up, I stop. I can't sing, and she probably thinks I'm being sacrilegious besides. Still kneeling, I slide open one of the doors behind the counter, begin inserting the bark at the back of the tray, behind what's already there.

Carrie is holding a chunk of rock candy aloft, analyzing it, turning it so that the flat edges catch the light and glint. She holds the candy to her nose and sniffs, scratches the surface with her fingernail and watches the sugar dust sparkle to the floor. She sniffs again. We went to the same grade school, but she was a year ahead of me, so I never really knew her until I started working here. I only knew that she was an O'Shaunessey. "This smells like nothing," she says.

"Maybe that's how rocks smell," I say.

She reaches a hand into the cabinet and selects a Jordan almond, an almond covered with a pink shell. "Bite this for me," she says, and I do, my tongue tasting the glossy sweetness, my teeth hesitating on the hard surface, then clamping down, crunching in. I hand her the half that's not in my mouth, and she smells it for half a minute, a minute, looking like she's breathing in pure happiness. Meanwhile, I flip the hard candy chips around with my tongue. I grind and chew, and the nutmeat turns mealy in my mouth.

Carrie smiles faintly with her eyes closed, her face as glazed and peaceful as an Easter ham. "Nice and roasty, toasty." Holding her hand over the wastebasket, she opens her fingers, and candy strikes metal with a clunk. She's been here since four o'clock, since right after school, and by now the bottom of the wastebasket is gory with mutilated candy.

"Is it good?" she asks.

I shrug and swallow. "I wouldn't pay money for it."

"No," she says, "but someone will."

Leaning against the counter, chins resting on folded hands, we watch the scanty foot traffic, the smattering of shoppers wandering through the courtyard. Carrie sighs pointedly, but I ignore her.

Out past the borders of Madeline's, the floor is covered with clay tiles that are not quite gold and not quite orange. Not quite shiny either. The walls are decorated with Spanish-style mosaics: bullfighters and flamenco dancers. It's hard to remember that this building used to be a Sears store. Four years ago, the automotive department was right here, shelves of motor oil and air filters; on Saturdays I would come here with my dad, whine and mope and look at hubcaps. Now the building is full of snooty little stores that sell turquoise jewelry and women's shoes.

Twenty feet away, at the center of the courtyard, the fountain
splashes too vigorously, sloshes wishing water onto the floor. Every
few weeks a plumber comes in to lower the volume and sop up the
puddles. People—kids and shoppers—looking down from the upper
levels like to aim pennies toward the fountain; once one landed on my
head as I was walking by. I was startled, but I didn't look up, didn't
want to see a bunch of laughing, staring boys. Reaching to retrieve the
coin, I made my own wish, threw the penny in the fountain, kept on
walking.

Carrie sighs again. "If it stays this slow, I might leave," she says and
scrutinizes me, trying to read my reaction. I nod and wish for customers—even cranky, pushy customers would be okay—but I don't
say anything. On weekday nights we work in twos—for bathroom
reasons primarily. But Carrie has worked here so long she can set her
own schedule, make her own rules. I certainly can't make her stay,
but if she's waiting for me to say, "Go on, go ahead," well, I'm not going to do that either.

"Of course, I could use the money." She crosses her arms in front
of herself and stands there in her pink smock and brown corduroys,
trying to decide between freedom and minimum wage.

The security guard paces the ground floor from McDonald's to the
front door. As he passes Madeline's he nods at us. He's always here,
the same guard, walking back and forth, making sure preteens don't
run up the escalators in the wrong direction. He's not so old, twenty-
three or twenty-four, and he seems nice enough—shy maybe—but
I've never said more than hi or hey or hello. He's black, and I wonder if that's the reason I don't talk to him. If this was a movie, he would
stop by twice a night and tease us into giving him candy, and we
would all be friends.

Not that it should matter—black or white. Of course it shouldn't
matter. The nicest person at my old job was black, a busboy named
Kenyatta. He was tall and friendly, handsome with an easy smile.
Once I slipped and spilled a tray, slopped two blueberry sundaes and

a pitcher of ice water on myself, right down my front, purple juice soaking through my clothes. Kenyatta took the tray from me and set it on a table, then he reached his arms around me, as if to hug me; he untied my apron and lifted the soggy, sticky cloth off me, and right there, right then, in the middle of the restaurant, I started to cry.

Carrie's arms drop to her sides. The choice has been made: she will stay, and I am immediately calmer, safer. She unzips her backpack, takes out a notebook, launches in. This is the homework for her religion class, a kind of religion diary that they have to do at her school. I don't bother to peek because I know she'll read the whole thing to me when she's done. She writes about how she feels when the priest raises the host up in the air—shivery—and how she thinks it's a sin not to help out around the house. I can't tell if she means what she writes or not. As for myself, I haven't been to church in the last five weeks, though I don't mention this fact to Carrie. Actually, no one knows. I pass the time in Dairy Queen, drinking diet sodas, hiding out.

You've got to understand who I am, who I used to be: for me to miss mass is no small matter. When I was a kid, I used to wait after church to pick up prayer cards out of the pews. I thought I could gather in holiness that way—as if prayer cards were collector's items, were valuable in some way. For so many years, I went to church every morning before school; I sat in the front and sang the songs. I believed in God and prayed and tried to live right, and at the end of each day, I reviewed my sins and near sins. I had a little book full of pictures of saints, drops of blood spilling down their faces—Rita and Rosa and Sebastian—I read their histories and tried to be like them. Bit by bit, though, I've lost all that—I've lost my hold on myself, lost my grip.

At Madeline's we sell five kinds of fudge and six kinds of nuts. I dig out a square of dense chocolate, press a cashew in, take a bite. Carrie stops writing and looks at me for a few seconds, her lips apart, like she's about to say something. With her staring at me—she's hardly even blinking—I feel a little self-conscious, but I keep eating. Once the taste of chocolate is in my mouth, I'm gone. Yes, I know the consequences: when I started here, Carrie told me about a girl who gained thirty pounds in a month and then quit. Chewing, I can hear my teeth clicking, gnashing—but I still can't stop.

"Don't eat that," she says. "You don't want that."

"Yes, I do." I swallow the sludgy mass, then lick my greasy lips. If I were alone now, I would eat another piece. I definitely would. But for now I clasp my hands; I contain myself.

Carrie flips back a few pages in her notebook. "How's this?" she asks and begins to read:

" 'The sacraments are our special moments with God. Of course, I can't remember being baptized, but I can imagine the water on my forehead and also the baptismal gown that my grandma sewed and the warm feeling of belonging to God.'

"Do you think that's okay?" she asks. " 'The warm feeling of belonging to God'? 'Warm'? Or should I say 'soft'?"

"Whichever," I say, and she continues:

" 'For first communion we dressed in white and walked in straight lines, and when I got to the front and looked at the priest, I was too shy to stick out my tongue. I didn't want him to see inside my mouth.'

"Wait a minute," she says and picks up her pen. She turns the notebook sideways and scribbles something along the margin. I think of my own first communion—my dress and the presents and the coconut cake in the shape of a lamb. I got a charm bracelet with two charms dangling—one for baptism, one for first communion. I loved that bracelet until I realized that it would be impossible to collect the charms for all the sacraments; I couldn't be a nun *and* get married, and I couldn't earn the charm for last rites until I was dead, until I was beyond bracelets.

Carrie starts in again. " 'My first confession wiped away my sins— baby sins like whispering a cuss word into my pillow! I walked around the whole day feeling fresh.' " She rests the top edge of the notebook against her lower lip, raises her eyebrows, and waits for my review.

92

The last part sounds like a deodorant commercial, but I'm not going to tell her that. "It's good," I say. "What was the question?"

But she doesn't answer; she turns her back to me. A customer: a boy.

He heads straight for Carrie, and I am nothing; I'm a piece of gravel on a driveway. Not that I should mind—I have a boyfriend, after all—but I can't help feeling frumpy and resentful.

It's weird, too. A few weeks ago Richie was talking about how he wouldn't mind being a priest—"I could help people," he said, "and I wouldn't have to ever worry about getting a job." We were sitting in the car, and he looked at me to see what I thought of the idea. I didn't say anything. What did he think I'd say?

The boy leans up against the counter and smiles at Carrie. He's wearing a T-shirt from the deli upstairs and a name tag that says Brady, but I don't know if that's his first name or his last name. I can't tell if Carrie knows him or not, but here is my observation, simple and true: when Carrie works, boys buy candy.

Carrie points at this and that in the display case, suggests different things he might buy. I watch them giggle and flirt. When the words come out of my mouth, I don't recognize my voice. "She doesn't kiss," I blurt, and Carrie and the boy stare at me. Immediately, I want to stuff the words back into my mouth. My face is burning, and I think of the time when I was four, when it was my sister's birthday party, and I stood up at the dinner table and pulled down my pants. My sister says that when I sat down, I laughed like a crazy person then started crying. I only remember red, raging embarrassment.

Carrie is like the outline of a chapter in a history book: I, II, III; a, b, c. I wonder if she ever screams, if she ever tells her mother she won't clean her room, won't scrub the bathtub. I wonder if she ever tells her mother to fuck off.

Now she reaches a hand into the candy counter and pulls out a skinny black licorice whip. The boy takes it obediently, gratefully, like a kid accepting a sucker from the grocery store checkout clerk. "Bye-

bye," she says to him, and he walks away, stopping once to look back. She waves, then turns to me.

I press my hands together, fingertips pointing toward the floor. Holy palmer's kiss, that's what I think of, that scene from *Romeo and Juliet* where they touch hands; we watched the movie in English class. But that's a love scene, and I'm all alone.

Of course she'll leave now. Of course.

"I was trying to be funny," I say.

"You were trying to be mean." She pushes her hand into her front pants pocket and pulls out a dollar bill folded small. "Do me a favor," she says. "Get me a yogurt."

So this is my penance: to walk humbly after the deli boy, to bow my head and buy her a yogurt. Luckily Brady isn't in sight when I get there, and someone else takes the money, another deli boy. Since Carrie didn't tell me what kind to get, I choose peach, a flavor I think she'll like, and when the yogurt passes from my hand to hers, we seem to be friends, or at least friendly co-workers, which is what we were before.

Nonetheless, at nine o'clock her boyfriend, Allan, arrives to take her away. He is just as you'd imagine—handsome, with perfect features and perfect hair and a green polo shirt tucked into neat khaki trousers.

Inside my head I offer up a fierce, pleading, quiet prayer—Don't leave, please don't leave—before I remember that I don't believe in praying, that it's no longer an option.

Carrie shakes her finger at me. "No more candy," she says, and I'm not sure whether she's trying to be funny or mean. I want to grab hold of her wrist, force her to drag me along behind her. But they're already gone, off to hold hands and be happy.

And I am here, all alone.

A wad of paper towels and a spray bottle, and I'm cleaning the windows of the case, rubbing away smudges, fingerprints, nose prints. I don't have to do this. It's not like I'll get a certificate, a little ribbon—employee of the month!

When I finish the windows, I wipe down the scales, the cash register, the fudge machine.

Do you know the fudge at Madeline's comes from a mix? The first person here in the morning pours in the powder, quickly, furtively, and plugs in the big electric fudge pot. At Soren's Ice House, the restaurant where I used to work, we opened industrial-sized cans of clam chowder and minestrone and called the soup homemade. "If anyone asks, say it's 'home-style,' " the manager instructed. I loved the job anyway, running around in my floppy, comfy waitress moccasins, bringing ice cream in glass goblets, rushing to get the orders out before it all melted. After closing we changed the radio from easy listening to KSOL, the black station, and we wiped the tables and put up the chairs, sang along to Earth, Wind, and Fire and "Rapper's Delight."

But then one day the cash register came up short—a hundred dollars missing—and everything got confusing. I quit—resigned, they called it. Whatever it was, I don't work there anymore. The new policy said that everyone on the shift had to chip in to cover the shortfall—a hundred dollars split five ways. Since I was on the shift, I would have to pay. But I couldn't pay, shouldn't have to pay; didn't, I repeat, did not take the money. And so I walked, jingle, slam, out into the heat of five o'clock in July, out and away from the other workers, my friends, their faces showing shock and anger, their brains still adding and subtracting, adjusting, deciding.

Do you know how long I worked at Soren's? Do you know how hard? Do you know what it's like to scoop ice cream for eight hours—rum raisin as soft as goulash and rocky road like digging into the side of a mountain—bending and scraping and people's tempers getting shorter and shorter?

I stumbled blotchy faced and crying through the crowded streets of the Plaza, thought of the old black woman who came in once a week and ordered one scoop of strawberry and one scoop of vanilla. I thought of how she hugged me when she came into the store; how she wouldn't let anyone else wait on her.

I thought of Michael, one of the boys who worked behind the fountain, making malts and shakes and sundaes. He kept his hair shaved close and talked about how he could get excused from any class to go lift weights for football. When he worked the fountain at Soren's, he was like an artist; his scoops were beautifully round, and they always weighed exactly a quarter of a pound. His muscles bulged as he drew the dipper across the surface of a tub of ice cream.

Good-bye, Michael; good-bye, old lady.

Do you know they found the missing money the next day, a hundred-dollar bill caught up in some cranny in the cash register's mechanism. Michael told me when I slipped in one morning for my check. They found the money, but no one ever called me to apologize, to ask me to come back.

I scoop a pound of chocolate malt balls; they tumble into the bag with a shuffling, hollow sound like peanut shells, like mice skittering. I hand the bag to a middle-aged couple, collect their money. I don't even smile. I'm nobody to them, just a dull candy girl in a pink smock and brown pants. At Soren's I smiled all day, all night, and felt my pockets getting heavier and heavier with money.

At a minute after ten, I'm closed inside the storeroom. My heart is thumping. Above me, around me, are rows and rows of neat white boxes. Slashes and circles, symbols and codes.

And I almost walk away, almost grit my teeth and walk away; almost grip the doorknob, walk away. I imagine how it would feel to be clean and unencumbered: breezes would blow across the courtyard as I passed through, balloons would drift down from the ceiling, roses would fall from the sky. I would be pure and free and happy.

But it's not that easy. It's simply not that easy.

I shake open a big white shopping bag and begin to pull boxes down from the shelves—Ch. Prtz., Cara., Hore. Drps., Tof. Brs. And I start throwing candy in: anything, everything.

Of course, I shouldn't be doing this. Of course, of course, of course. Another box, heave-ho, a shower of bright green sourballs. When I put the box back up, I touch the surrounding boxes to make sure that they're properly positioned, not too far forward or too far back. Just so, everything just so. I brush some grains of sugar off the countertop, empty my hand into the wastebasket. My heart is still pounding, and my face is red; I can feel how hot my cheeks are. If Carrie came back now—just say she forgot her notebook, her wallet—if Carrie came back, I would die. I would try to cram myself into one of these boxes. I would turn myself into a rock.

If I took this bag out front, if I weighed it on the scale, I might get scared, might put everything back. Not that it matters, not that anyone will ever care or know or check. This store is just here as a convenience to the Bammans, the rich family that owns it. For their parties we pack up ten-pound boxes of chocolates, wrap them in silver paper, send the boxes to the house—the penthouse, the mansion, whatever it is.

Do you know that the owner at Soren's—Leslie Carmichael—used to be a ballerina in New York? On Saturday mornings we had employee meetings before the store opened, and she told us that she wanted a fur coat; she wanted to retire when she was forty. We weren't supposed to clock in for the meetings, and it made me so mad. When I left my house, I'd always promise myself that I'd punch in, but I never did.

Still, how to explain the time she came to a football game at my high school and watched me perform with the drill team at halftime?

Inside the bag the candy is all in a jumble; it looks like some kind of crazy casserole my mother might dream up. Sourballs wedged into the twists of the pretzels. At home my family will dig in; they will eat and eat and so will I until I am sick and bloated and miserable.

They'll stuff their mouths with candy, chew and chew and never ask. They'll eat and eat and never ask.

I load the bag, more and more, and the walls of the storeroom seem to push closer, all those little white boxes take a tiny step forward, and I try to shrink myself smaller, disappear inside myself.

I shouldn't be doing this. I should stop myself, but it's like the dream I have where I bite down too hard on my teeth, and they begin to crumble, and I can't stop biting. I can't stop until my teeth are jagged edges, until my mouth is full of powder.

Leslie Carmichael will never call me; she'll never admit she was wrong. And Carrie won't come back and discover me, won't scold me and set me straight. I know I'm on my own.

Last year I went on a retreat—it was my idea to go, not my mother's or anyone else's. I filled out the forms myself, sent in the money, recruited my friend Anna to go with me. During that weekend, I felt charged up, ignited, though I'm suspicious of those sensations now; they came, I think, from too little sleep, from the buzz of meeting new people. We talked in small groups, and in one discussion a girl confessed that she'd had sex—"a *lot*"—and she said she was sorry. She cried so long I thought she might never stop. One by one the people in the group went over and hugged her, and she sobbed and thanked us. I put my arms around her when it seemed to be my turn.

I didn't tell my own secrets then, that a month before a policeman had seen me naked on the top level of a parking garage, had come sirens screaming up to the car where I sat making out with Richie. The policeman pointed his flashlight and looked at me for a long, long time. "What's going on here?" he asked. "There's been a report of a rape in progress." I sat in stunned silence—he was staring at me; I knew he was staring at me. He flipped his thumb toward the adjacent apartment building. "Ought to bother you," he said, "people looking out their windows and seeing you." Then he asked our names and wrote them on a piece of paper and took them away. Afterward, I wouldn't talk to Richie, wouldn't even look at him.

I didn't tell this story to the group, though it came into my mind. The grand finale of the retreat was a mass where friends and family came through a back door and surprised us. Laughing, crying, noise and balloons. Everyone was hugging their parents and friends, but I didn't see anyone for me. I was standing by a boy I'd met, a soft-spoken basketball player who'd driven in from a small college in Kansas. No one had come for him either, so by default we hugged each other. When he stepped away, he was crying, but I saw my parents then, and I left him standing all alone. His name was David—I remember his name.

Driving home I felt great, alive and full of love, but Anna predicted that the feelings would wear off. "We'll go back to school," she said, "and the locker will get stuck, and we'll be our usual mean, bad selves." And she was right. Day by day my happy feeling dwindled until it finally was gone. It wasn't any one thing, no bolt from heaven. Do I have to have a reason?

I wonder what would happen if I walked out of here with five of these boxes, so many boxes that I couldn't see ahead of me, so many boxes piled in my arms that the guard would have to help me. Would he open the door or would he stop me? Would I find myself in some rinky-dink Plaza security office, calling my parents to come get me, waiting for the police to show up and ask me things? I would sit in a straight-backed chair, and three detectives would stand around me, like in the movies, and they would poke and prod and drag everything out of me. Would I tell the truth or would I lie, inventing crimes, inventing guilt? Would I confess to stealing money from the register at Soren's? I wouldn't steal money. I wouldn't. I didn't. Remember, they found the money. They found it, a crummy, wrinkled hundred-dollar bill. Remember?

The boxes stare down at me with slits and slashes, beady black eyes. I'll tell you—should I tell you? There are other secrets I could tell, old secrets. Once I was baby-sitting at the Fishes', and the baby, Andy, was howling, crying and crying. Constant, terrible screaming, and he made me want to scream, too. Once in a while, a hole would open in the noise—a few seconds of tense, ragged silence, and he would pinch his face together small and tight and so ugly, flame red, crazy red. When I tried to push the nipple of the bottle into his mouth, he got madder— louder. I was eleven, think of that—in your mind give me braids and a Holly Hobby T-shirt. I gripped the bottle, pale blue plastic with an inch of tepid milk sloshing at the bottom. I held the bottle, and he was screaming, and I rapped him with it. I did, right on the head. As soon as I did it, I was scared, so scared—had I hit a soft spot, had I made him retarded? Maybe it was only a tap, maybe not much harder than a kiss. I can't remember, can't be sure. By the time the Fishes came home, he had stopped crying, had fallen into an exhausted sleep, his little chest heaving and shuddering. I told the parents about the cry-ing, but not about the bottle. They paid me four dollars, and we stood together at the side of the crib and watched him sleep.

I am trembling now, pushing soft sweetness into my mouth, chew-ing, swallowing. I am eating everything I find. I don't know what I'm eating, don't know what I'm doing.

I kept baby-sitting there because they didn't know. They liked me. I was baby-sitting again, and Andy was older, a year and a half or two years old, and I was changing his diaper. Maybe I was twelve now, or thirteen. He was on the bed upstairs, legs flying in the air, piss and ammonia and baby smell all around, and his little penis was there, so small and strange, and I just wondered what it was like to have sex, what it would be like, and I put my arms on either side of him, and I lowered them like I was doing a push-up, stopped a couple of inches above him, thinking that it wouldn't really be like this, but something like this, then I pushed myself away. That's all I did—that's all, a few inches away, just to help me imagine. I didn't do anything, but Andy's eyes were big and scared looking, and round as planets.

Sometimes now I walk past their house, and I see Andy grown tall and skinny, seven years old, riding his bike, and I don't know whether to say hi or not. I don't know if he remembers me.

Do you know I sat in the parking lot at Loose Park last April and split a box of Mystic Mints with my friend Anna, one by one by row by row, every last cookie, then I smelled the box and wanted more. My stomach felt stretched and awful and I wanted more. I scraped up chocolate with my fingernail. Then Anna told me what she did, what she had done since eighth grade, hid in the bathroom and made herself vomit, tried to make herself skinny. She made me promise not to tell anyone; she asked if I could help her. But I didn't know what to say, or do. A couple of months later, I asked her if she still did it, and she said no, not too much, and that's where it stands. She told me her secret, and I did nothing. A couple of weeks ago, she asked me to bring her fudge, and I did.

I know Carrie has secrets, too—besides the ones she tells. Her older brother came back from Vietnam and then killed himself. That was several years ago—I remember the whispers in school—but she's never said a word about it. Secrets and sins: when her friends from school come by, Carrie gives them candy—she shouldn't do that. And she shouldn't waste candy the way she does. She certainly isn't perfect. But nothing touches her, nothing reaches her, and I wish that I could be her: pristine and wrapped in cellophane and satisfied with sniffing.

A peanut butter cup is gone before you realize you've eaten it, peel back the paper and swallow it down. The little brown paper holders spot the counter, dark and wrinkled things—I think old women's nipples might look like this, but I've never seen an old woman's breast. Ten, fifteen, twenty, I crush the papers in my hand, toss the ball into the trash. Does the guard wonder anything? Does he know? Usually by now, I've pulled down the gates, I've turned out the lights, I've nodded good night at the door. If I was in here until midnight, would he check on me, would he knock on the door, ask if I was okay?

The guard looks like the kind of person who goes to church on Sundays and lives with his mother. I'll bet she makes him mashed potatoes for dinner, washes and folds his laundry.

I wish my mother would fold my wash. I wish she would come in here and take my hand and lead me away.

I ease out of the storeroom and lock the door, then I use the long metal pole to crank down the gates that surround and protect the counter. When the gate is halfway down, I hang the pole back on its hook and duck under. Then I push down on the chains, putting the weight of my body into the motion, until the gate slams against the tiles.

The fountain splashes in the background, and I heft my white bag the size of a pillow, the size of a suitcase. I walk slowly.

Isn't it obvious? Won't someone stop me?

Arms full of candy, I walk toward the door, toward the no-name guard who paces back and forth. When I get close enough, he will open the door for me. He will know what I'm doing, and he'll let me go.

In the downstairs kitchen, Jessie touched Alma's arm and told her the words that were written there: "It's one thing to sing the beloved."

"What does it mean?" Alma asked.

Jessie shrugged. "I only know what it says."

In the days and nights after, Alma repeated the words and stretched her mind toward their meaning, the way old women in churches touch their rosaries and find God.

From the steps of the Miller-O'Malley Dance Studio, Alma watched the protesters who had gathered across the street. She'd driven the short distance to Cheryl's Beauty Plus and then parked several blocks away; in the end she walked almost as far as the distance from her home to the beauty parlor. But she'd seen the movies where people cross picket lines and get their heads smashed with baseball bats, and she wanted the safety of her car.

The weather had been cool so far this summer—she'd heard that volcanoes were to blame. Today she wore a light blue jogging suit with a sleeveless turtleneck under the jacket. For once, the rash on her arms was calm; she thought maybe the fleecy fabric was a soothing influence. Across Cherry Street, the milling, shuffling crowd seemed abstract—color and motion. The passing traffic muffled words, coughs, sneezes, all human sounds. The scene made Alma think of an anthill, protesters and ants both driven by a purpose she didn't understand.

Only Jessie stood still, rooted at the curb as if she had been planted there. Alma wondered if someone had guided Jessie to that spot or if she'd somehow found it herself. Since the day Jessie had moved into the apartment on the third floor of Alma's house, Alma had been observing her carefully. Two years later, Alma still puzzled over how Jessie was able to navigate, to manage, without being able to see. Jessie's long, light brown hair drifted and floated, and occasionally the wind lifted her skirt and swirled the filmy fabric around her legs. With one hand, she held a sign that said, "Shame, Shame"; her other hand was curled loosely around her long, white cane.

Just behind Jessie, Alma could see the big front window of Cheryl's Beauty Plus—the shock of red paint across the glass. Alma couldn't believe people could be so mean, so destructive. And then they stood around bragging about it—"claiming responsibility," they called it. What they should claim, Alma thought, was irresponsibility.

Alma watched as Cheryl's daughter, Sue, pushed the front door open and stepped out, guiding an elderly woman. The protesters made space for Sue and the woman to walk through, then closed in tight again. After tucking the woman into the car, Sue squared her shoulders and cleared all expression from her face. The protesters didn't move this time, and Sue had to turn sideways and slice a path between the bodies with her shoulder.

The trouble at Beauty Plus had started less than a week before, when Cheryl made what seemed to Alma a simple and inevitable decision: she fired Martin. Alma couldn't begin to remember how long Martin had been cutting hair at Beauty Plus; she couldn't guess how many times she'd heard him and Cheryl trying to decide what to do about lunch—pizza or ribs, or should they just hold off until dinner? Of course, Cheryl hadn't wanted to fire him, but what choice did she have with Martin so weak he could hardly hold the scissors?

Martin was definitely strange, obviously fruity, but Alma had always liked him. Once or twice, she'd watched his late-night show—part talk show, part seance—on public access television. He sat with his guests at a bare table and said things like, "I hear your mother. I feel her spirit, and what she wants is for you to be happy. She wants you to get the dog." Alma's husband, Chuck, had seen the show, too, and whenever Alma came home from a hair appointment, he would ask, "Is this a voodoo hairdo?" Martin was a gentle man, though, and conscientious—he never left her stranded under the dryers, and he always remembered that she didn't like hair spray.

But now that Martin was so sick, Alma sympathized with Cheryl. Once Alma had had to fire an employee who missed too many days at the Floral Shoppe at Super Food Barn. She certainly hadn't liked doing it, but she needed a worker she could count on. Beauty Plus was a tiny operation—just three chairs—and even before anyone knew it was AIDS, Martin's coughing was keeping customers away. He still did good work, but after her last damp, depressing appointment, Alma herself had made the decision to get her hair done on Martin's day off.

And now Jessie, knowing none of the history and none of the facts, had taken up Beauty Plus as her cause. That was Jessie, thought Alma. If people were protesting, Jessie was out there, carrying a sign and marching in circles. Jessie always had an opinion. She was for wilderness preserves, against war, for abortion, against high-voltage electricity lines. She was always giving Alma pamphlets full of cartoons that weren't funny, and photocopied articles clipped from newspapers

Alma had never heard of. Once or twice a week, Jessie came down-stairs carrying a sign, headed for a rally. If the sign faced outward, Alma would look to see what it said, but if the sign was reversed, she didn't ask.

Alma thought of the conversation she'd had two nights ago, when Jessie stopped in the living room to listen to the TV news—a segment on Bosnia; an update on the situation at Beauty Plus.

At the commercial, Alma turned off the sound and watched the picture, people riding horses and drinking soda.

"Christ," said Jessie, shaking her head. "It's not 1982 anymore. Hasn't anyone learned anything?"

"Nobody wants to get AIDS," Alma defended. "Nobody wants to get coughed on."

"Alma!" Jessie's thin, pale arms flew up in exasperation. The tip of her long cane snagged in the carpeting. "You don't get AIDS from someone coughing! Don't you see how illogical that thinking is? If that were the case, we'd all have AIDS. It simply doesn't spread that way."

"No one knows for sure. What about that dentist in Florida? Everyone said that was impossible. A billion to one."

"Listen, Alma. If you just looked at some up-to-date material, you'd see that you're entirely wrong. You're choosing to stay igno-rant."

"I believe what I believe," Alma had said. "And besides, people cut themselves with scissors, razors, whatever—barbers do it all the time, I've seen it. It's a dangerous business."

"Well," Jessie had said. "We disagree." Then she turned and marched upstairs. Alma had been both startled and relieved; it was one of the few times when Jessie didn't linger awkwardly at the end of a conversation.

Alma didn't need a haircut yet—less than four weeks had passed since her last one—but she called Cheryl's shop anyway. Jessie wasn't the only one who could protest.

"I hope you know what you're getting into," said Cheryl.

"I do," said Alma. "I'm tough."

Past the protesters, down the block, a group of children in swim-suits—four- and five-year-olds—emerged from Brookside Country Day. Holding hands, two by two, the children skipped and dawdled along the sidewalk, headed for the pool on Jasper. The boys all wore their towels as capes, à la Batman, except for one boy who carried his rolled up like a diploma. The girls transported their towels in varied and creative ways—as veils, skirts, purses. Alma stood quickly and hurried to the stoplight at the corner. She would try to slip into the beauty shop in the confusion created by the children. But by the time she got across the street, the children had already passed the protest-ers. The teachers, teenage girls with deep tans and green eye shadow, stopped the children at the light and counted heads. "Chaz!" one of the teachers said sharply. "Hold hands!"

Alma took a breath and kept walking. She felt the eyes of the crowd watching her. They seemed to know she wasn't one of them. Her legs grew syrupy and unstable. Her rear end felt enormous. Her face burned.

Jessie stood with her face tilted skyward, warming herself in the sun. Alma debated with herself. Should she say something to Jessie? "Hello, Jessie," touch her arm, then open the door, slip inside? Jessie would wonder who had spoken, or Jessie would know. Which? Maybe Jessie would recognize the sound of Alma's tennis shoes on the pavement.

There are twenty-one people, thought Alma. I will walk past them all. To choose a hairdresser is my right as a citizen and a tax-payer. I will walk past Jessie, and she will never know. I will go in-side. I will get my hair cut. Nearing the doorway, Alma had to weave and push. She wished she had made her own sign, one that told how Cheryl spent two afternoons a week going to the homes of old women who were too feeble to come to the store. Cheryl chatted, prettied them up, made them feel human again. Someone should write that on a sign.

At the door, a very tall man with a tiny goatee said, "Don't patronize homophobia," and looked her straight in the eyes. Someone else tried to slip a leaflet into her hand. From a few feet away came Jessie's voice, "Shame, shame."

No one was physically blocking the doorway, but Alma stood still on the sidewalk. She wanted to grab Jessie's arm and shake it; she wanted to say, "You! Shame, shame, you!" What did Jessie know? Nothing but what other people told her. Jessie couldn't even look in the window and see how hard Cheryl worked, on her feet for ten hours a day. Alma knew from experience how tiring that was. All Jessie could do was stand on the curb and hold up a paper sign that she couldn't even read. She didn't know the first thing.

The door to Beauty Plus swung open. Cheryl reached out her hand. "Come right in, Alma," she said in a loud, friendly voice. "We're all ready for you," and then Alma was safely enclosed in a warm, busy room that smelled strongly of hair spray and green apple shampoo.

On Alma's arm the words floated and meant nothing. She could hardly hold on to them, could hardly keep them following one after another. It's one thing to sing the beloved.

That night, standing in the basement, Alma hung the last of Chuck's shirts, then opened the dryer and checked the socks, pushing them back in as the machine spun slower and slower. Almost done. She moved her finger to the start button, then stopped before pressing it. In what should have been silence, she heard a noise, a sound of movement just past the furnace. Chuck was in St. Louis, and someone was here; someone was in the basement. Alma froze, uncertain of what she should do. Should she call out? Should she hide? Just last week a man had walked into a Mary Kay party on the next block, waved a gun, grabbed purses, ran out. Friends of hers had lost checkbooks, driver's licenses, cash. Patty Kelly lost a hundred dollars and a pearl necklace that she'd tucked into her handbag.

In the shadows, a shape appeared, moving slowly, shuffling closer. Alma held her breath, held tightly to the air in her lungs. The rash stampeded across her arms; she gripped the edges of the washing machine. Crouching, she pressed her body close to the cold metal. Oh, God, she prayed. Oh, God.

Inching her head forward, she watched and waited. Then she exhaled, loosened her fingers. Jessie.

Alma stood and stepped into the open. "Jessie, my goodness. You scared me!"

Among the basement clutter, a gray metal cabinet stood with the doors flung open, fishing rods and hip waders spilling out. Jessie had one hand on the side of the cabinet; from her other hand dangled a white plastic bag.

"I brought my trash down," said Jessie. "But I took a wrong turn somewhere. Isn't tomorrow trash day?"

"Here," said Alma. "It is. I'll put yours with the rest." She stacked the bag with the other trash. With nothing in her hands, Jessie looked frail and wispy thin, like a fourteen-year-old girl, ten years younger than she really was. "I mean it, Jessie. Leave your trash at the basement door, and I'll bring it down." Alma imagined Jessie wandering through the basement, cutting herself on a sharp corner or plunging her hand into a coffee can full of nails. "If you got lost," said Alma, "it might be two days before anyone thought to look down here."

"Well, I feel like I'm responsible for the trash I make."

"It's no trouble. It's easier than organizing a search party." Alma smiled, but Jessie couldn't see. In the laundry corner of the basement, the dryer buzzed, signaling the end of the cycle.

Upstairs, they sat together at the kitchen table, where Alma had never asked Jessie to sit before. The chairs were upholstered in green vinyl—the color had made more sense in one of the kitchen's earlier eras. The curtains were brown with beige lace; the linoleum was crisscrossed with short black lines made by falling knives. Alma hadn't looked critically at the kitchen for many years, and she wanted, suddenly, to apologize.

"Here's cookies." Alma set the plate down noisily, so Jessie could find it. "Store brand. Nothing fancy." For several seconds they sat in awkward silence. Alma fingered the clipped ends of her hair. She thought of that morning, of Jessie's voice floating over the mumble of the crowd: "Shame, shame." Did she know? wondered Alma. Did Jessie know?

Inside Beauty Plus, Martin's station had been cleared out, his jars of clips and combs gone. His chair was piled with towels. Cheryl had cut and cut, stopping only to make angry jabs in the air with her scissors, and Alma had sat quietly, watching her hair fall into her lap.

"There you go," said Cheryl at the end of it all. "A new you."

"Cute," Alma had said, using a hand mirror to see her head from different angles. She gave Cheryl a small, strained smile. Tilting her hand, Alma tried to use the mirror to study the crowd outside, but all she could see were street signs and bright sun.

Jessie ran a finger over the surface of the kitchen table.

"It looks like wood, but it's not," said Alma. "It's not as pretty as real wood, but it's easier to take care of. Would you like a banana or some cheese?"

"No, thanks," said Jessie.

Alma wondered if she should describe the kitchen to Jessie, the way people in movies described sunsets to their blind friends. She wondered if there were smells that told Jessie this was a kitchen and not a bedroom. Could she smell the glass of orange juice Alma had poured that morning? Could she smell a bedspread? A bathrobe? Could she smell the green apple fragrance of Alma's fresh haircut?

"I remember you used to have that player piano," said Jessie. "We'd practically be standing up to pump the pedals."

"It's still there," said Alma. "It's broken, though—no real reason to get it fixed. Nobody ever plays it."

"Your kids are all grown up."

Jessie lifted her head as if she was examining the ceiling, and Alma watched her. Should she tell Jessie that the ceiling was spackled, roughly textured with glitter sprinkled here and there? Did spackle matter? In the movies, blind people asked to feel their friends' faces, but Jessie had never done that.

If Jessie asked, Alma wondered, would I let her?

Alma reached to the middle of the table, and as she lifted a cookie off the plate, her arm brushed Jessie's hand, and Jessie kept her fingers there. "What's this?" she asked, gently touching the bumpy patch on Alma's arm.

"A rash. Maybe a food allergy. I don't know. It comes and goes."

Jessie continued to sweep her fingers along the bumps. She started at the edge closest to Alma's wrist, then sent her fingers flying along, like a pianist giving a flourish at the end of a song.

Alma didn't pull her arm away. She blinked and watched, paralyzed, amazed. "That tickles," she said, though it didn't really.

"Too weird," said Jessie. "Very weird."

"What is?"

"Your arm. I can read words on your arm." She cocked her head and looked into space, touching Alma's arm again and again. Alma smiled nervously and waited. "It's one thing to sing the beloved," said Jessie.

"That's what my arm says?"

"It seems to."

"How can it?" Jessie kept her fingers on Alma's forearm, just above the wrist. Alma shivered and watched the hairs on her arm stand straight.

"Maybe it's like a million monkeys at a million typewriters."

"My arm?"

"You know how some people get radio signals through their teeth?"

"It's just a rash," said Alma. She pulled her arm back and didn't look at it. "It's nothing to get excited about."

"Maybe," said Jessie.

Alma stared, trying to read the expression on Jessie's face—her lips were pulled into a straight line, her eyes made small, jerky movements, left-right, up-down. She didn't seem to be joking.

"What does it mean?" asked Alma.

Jessie shook her head. "I only know what it says."

*T*hat night, lying in bed, Alma listened to footsteps and voices overhead, the strumming and singing of Jessie and her friends. She thought of a news article that Jessie had given her a few months before—the article, smeared and folded, told of Guatemalan factories, rickety greenhouses where flowers grew in chemicals instead of dirt. The women who tended the flowers developed sores and ulcers and terrible cancers. "This is how we get flowers so cheaply in America," Jessie had said, standing in the entry hall, her long hair loose, fanned out across her back. "You ought to know about this. You're part of it."

Alma thought of the refrigerated display cases at work, the white plastic tubs crowded with daisies, roses, carnations. She thought of the Guatemalan women, hunched and weak, working among the perfect blooms. Eventually Alma had to open her eyes to stop the flowers from crowding in. She punched her pillow and kicked at the sheets. She wished Chuck had planned to come home tonight, not tomorrow. Upstairs, Jessie strummed her guitar. Outside, dogs barked, and police helicopters flew overhead and flooded the backyards with light. Alma prayed they would find the people they were searching for.

As a child Louis Braille poked his eye with a cobbler's awl, and the infection spread to his other eye. His parents sent him to a school for blind children, and there he developed his raised alphabet, the system of ordered dots that came to be known as braille. He punched his alphabet into the paper with an awl, the

same instrument that had blinded him. Alma looked in the B vol-
ume of the encyclopedia, read the article, studied the diagram.
The bumps on her arm were nothing like the dots pictured on the
page; her rash was ragged and imprecise. Still, she wondered.

Alma and Chuck had been surprised when Jessie called two years ago; they hadn't even been planning to rent out the third floor. They hadn't seen Jessie for years, but thanks to photocopied Christmas letters, they knew she had gone to college in Iowa. Now she was planning to settle in Kansas City, and she needed a reasonable, safe apartment on the bus line.

Years ago, when Jessie's father had worked with Chuck, the families had been friendly. Alma's children had been fascinated with the idea and the equipment of blindness—tape recorders, dulcimers, scratch-and-sniff books—but eventually Jessie had grown tired of people exclaiming over her things. Once, when Alma asked to see Jessie's braille watch, Jessie—no older than eight or ten—had put out her arm and wearily flipped the lid up. "I know it's interesting to you," she said, demonstrating, "but to me it's just ordinary."

When Jessie called, she said she remembered playing upstairs with Chuck and Alma's children. "We jumped on the beds," she said. "We wrapped ourselves in blankets and rolled down the stairs." (People were always telling Alma things that had happened on the third floor over the years. Bunk-bed parachutes and pissing contests.) Jessie also remembered that the rooms had been rented out for a time, to a young law student and his wife. Now that the kids were grown and gone, would Chuck and Alma be interested in renting to her?

They thought it over. Why not? Before everything was finalized, Chuck and Alma had debated whether to add a clause into the lease prohibiting overnight guests. They didn't want to meet unshaven men in the early morning hours. But they decided against it, not wanting Jessie to feel they were accusing her of something she might not have even considered doing. As it turned out, Jessie had lots of friends, but no one who seemed like a boyfriend. Most of Jessie's friends were women.

For Alma, living with Jessie was educational, like having an exchange student from Sweden or El Salvador. Alma watched and learned—she was ready to help, but Jessie almost never asked. At the grocery store, Jessie got the manager to accompany her through the aisles. Friends helped her with bills. She rode the bus everywhere, fearlessly walking in neighborhoods that Alma wouldn't go into with five fierce German shepherds. In the first weeks that Jessie lived with Chuck and Alma, an assistant from the Society for the Blind had come to show her around the city and help her plot out her life. Chuck did the same thing inside the house, showing Jessie where all the cabinets were, where the ceiling sloped, how the toilet flushed, how to lock the doors.

In time, Alma got used to Jessie's friends walking through the house on the way to Jessie's apartment. She got used to keeping the stairs clear of shoes and newspapers and stray sweaters. For Alma, the enduring problem was conversation—she dreaded talking to Jessie. She was an interesting, friendly girl, yet somehow every conversation was eternal and awkward, even the simplest "Hello, how are you." Jessie couldn't read yawns and fidgets, couldn't tell when a connection had broken down. "So anyway," Alma would say, and still Jessie would remain, half smiling, leaning forward on her cane. In the middle of the silence that should have been the end, Jessie would introduce a new topic—"Did you barbecue last night?"—and they'd stand around for ten more minutes, talking about brisket. Sometimes Alma would glance at newspaper headlines while they talked. She'd finally had to resort to inventing errands. Once she said, "Excuse me, I have to check the roast in the oven." It was only later that she remembered that Jessie could smell, even if she couldn't see.

When Alma told Chuck, he laughed. "Next time," he told her, "you can say, 'There's the phone, excuse me.' "

"You're terrible," said Alma.

"Who's terrible?"

Alma said nothing.

"Who?" said Chuck.

Once Alma had been sitting in the living room when Jessie opened the front door and came in. As Jessie paused in the entry way, listening, Alma sat absolutely still on the couch, barely breathing, the magazine trembling in her hand. Time passed, then Jessie adjusted her backpack on her shoulder and headed upstairs, the old wood grumbling with each footstep. Alma sat so still she could hear Jessie's movements on the second floor; she could hear the key turn in the lock.

Once at a prayer meeting, Alma heard a woman speaking in tongues, in a language that sounded like church bells. Someone else translated the sounds into English, into words of praise, words of prayer, and the dingy, ill-lit room was alive with the spirit, with adrenaline. Later, when she told Chuck about the meeting, she couldn't describe the sounds, the energy, the feelings she'd had. She tried to say the words, but she couldn't capture the sounds. She felt like an idiot, speaking in squawks.

It was two days later, and Chuck was back from St. Louis. Alma, worn out from eight hours in the Floral Shoppe, sat beside him in the car. "I'm going to tell her we're moving," said Chuck. "I'll tell her the for-sale sign is up, and she's got a month."

"You'd rather move than ask her to be quiet?" Alma couldn't tell if Chuck was serious or just cranky.

Chuck grunted.

Jessie's music *was* too loud—Alma admitted that. She could count a hundred nights when Chuck lay in bed, tossing and complaining while Jessie played peace songs overhead.

"Don't be silly," said Alma. They couldn't just put a blind girl out on the street—especially not Jessie. She'd probably organize her friends to picket their house. Alma held her hands over the air-conditioner vents and dried the sweat with blasts of cold air.

"Nobody is going to buy with a crazy blind girl living upstairs," he said.

The stream of cold air tickled, and Alma itched. "People will understand that she's not part of the sale. Just like they know we're going to take the furniture and the curtains with us."

"What if someone wants to see the house? Will we be able to walk up there and check that everything's clean? Make sure the toilet's flushed?"

"For pity's sake, Chuck! This whole conversation is ridiculous—we're not selling the house."

Alma flipped the air vent shut, then folded her hands tightly on her lap. It was frightening to encounter Jessie in dark hallways, dark basements. Alma admitted that. And some of Jessie's friends were downright grungy. She met people at rallies and invited them over, and they had to walk right through Alma's house on their way to Jessie's apartment. And then there were the strange things Jessie said, her eyes restless, secretive, blank—it would be a relief to be rid of her. Yes.

But whatever Alma thought, whatever Chuck thought, they couldn't do anything. Because whatever they did, Jessie would know.

Alma balled her hands into fists. The rash was driving her crazy—or else she was already crazy, and there was no rash. She'd thought of that possibility. She touched a finger to her wrist, gave her arm a tiny scratch, and the frenzy of itching began.

She stretched the words like a rubber band, wrapped them twice around the world. She pulled, pulled—and the words snapped with incredible force, knocking her breathless, cutting her in half.

After dinner that night Alma left the dishes on the table—she wanted to get her walk in before dark, and besides, Chuck usually washed them if she left the house. The weather was warm, and when she went outside she found Jessie and her friend Karen sitting on the porch swing, sitting and hugging.

It wasn't the kind of hug that a friend gives to a friend. Alma saw that right away; she saw that something wasn't kosher. In the flash of an instant, rocking on the rubber soles of her walking shoes, Alma debated whether to say hello or go by. Jessie and Karen decided for her; they were so involved with each other that they didn't even notice her. Alma hurried down the stairs.

Before dinner she had put on a long-sleeved blouse, so Chuck wouldn't have to look at the angry red patches on her arms. But now, walking, long sleeves were a mistake. Sleeves brushing skin, rash tingling. Alma traveled her usual route through the neighborhood, racing dusk, fighting her desire to scratch. To distract herself, she looked at houses, at sidewalks. The trees were so beautiful and so green, a maple, a dogwood . . . no use. The rash was alive.

She'd been to the doctor once already, but the rash was fickle. As she readied herself for the appointment—showering, selecting a blouse—her forearm was livid with red dots. But an hour later, when she rolled up her sleeve in the examining room, the bumps were gone. "It's usually right here," she said lamely.

The doctor wrote notes into Alma's file. She wondered what he was writing there. Maybe some code word for hypochondria. Maybe she was reacting to strawberries or chocolate or some chemical residue on the flowers, the same poison that devastated the flower workers in Guamemala. "If the irritation reasserts itself, I'll prescribe a cream," said the doctor. "You can put your sleeve down again. Come back when the rash is active. Come back if you have any trouble."

Alma walked west on Fiftieth Terrace, toward the park. At Wornall, she stopped to look. The house on the corner, a Mediterranean-style villa, was enormous, a showplace in a neighborhood where big houses were common. She'd long admired the landscaping, the borders of red salvia. When her youngest boys were in junior high, they'd come over here to swim. "Who lives there?" Alma had asked, still trying to supervise their comings and goings, though there were whole chunks of their lives she knew nothing about.

"Two old guys," they told her. "They're fags. They sit on the patio and watch us swim."

"You find somewhere else to swim," Alma had commanded, though she had no way of checking to see that they obeyed.

She couldn't imagine the attraction, a man loving a man. Women loving women. What about children? Did they want the human race to just stop?

The house was empty now; Alma had heard from neighbors that both men had died of AIDS, both in the last month. Standing before the house, Alma thought of Martin. He would get thinner and sicker and sadder. It hadn't fully occurred to her until this moment that Martin would die; she hadn't thought it through. Someone would gather all his combs and throw them in the trash.

Maybe Cheryl was wrong, Alma thought. Maybe Jessie had been right to complain. Night was falling all around her. Alma took a slow breath then exhaled. There. Good. The rash had itched itself out. She turned and headed home.

Jessie and Karen had turned on the porch light, and Karen was laying out a deck of cards. They leaned forward toward the cards, but they weren't sitting as close as before. Still, Alma could see the shape of their earlier embrace; she remembered the black outlines of it, then she made herself forget.

"Alma!" Karen called.

Alma smiled. Of Jessie's friends, Karen was the only one who made an effort to stop and chat. She asked questions about Alma's flowers, told funny stories about Winston, her cat. Karen liked to cook and often gave samples to Alma, who was an appreciative audience. She was older than Jessie—close to thirty, Alma thought.

"You got a haircut," said Karen.

Alma could feel her face turning pink, but she tried to keep her voice steady. "It's too short," she said. "I'm not that happy with it." She wondered if Jessie was adding two and two. But Jessie just sat quietly, listening.

"It's cute," said Karen.

Alma pinched a few yellow leaves off the Swedish ivy. She pointed to the cards. "What's this?"

"Tarot. We're looking into Jessie's future." Karen placed a card. "The queen of cups." Karen's red hair fell in straight lines, concealing her face. In the porch light her hair was transformed into a golden helmet. "This is a good card. The queen sits on a throne at the edge of the sea. She gazes at a magnificent cup, and she seems to find meaning there, the way some people can look into a pool of water or a fire and see the truth."

Alma examined the card. The rocks were green and orange circles; the waves were black lines drawn into whirlpools; the cup seemed to have sprouted birds' wings.

"Some strong woman will help you achieve your desires. It could be your mother, a friend, an employer." Alma slapped a mosquito off her leg. In the shadowy parts of the yard, fireflies had begun to blink, hundreds of fireflies. Karen looked at Alma and smiled. "It could be your landlord."

"Goodness," Alma said quickly. "I don't think it's me."

Jessie tapped her fingers impatiently on Karen's knee. "Do the next card."

"This final card should sum up what we've learned so far," said Karen. "It's the chariot reversed."

Alma held her breath and hoped that Jessie would have a good future. To be blind seemed trouble enough.

Karen sat for a moment looking thoughtful. Then she pulled a small booklet out of the tarot card box. "I can't remember this one."

Jessie laughed. "Goofball."

"Hey, now," said Karen. "Be nice. I'm new at this."

With the dark and the locusts and the fireflies, Alma had been seeing possibilities in the cards, in the words. But now that Karen was thumbing through the instruction book, Alma saw the orange plastic pillows on the swing, the flutter of dead leaves from the spider plant. She thought of Jessie in the kitchen, Jessie touching her arm. Now, Jessie's eyes were shifting rapidly, looking nowhere. She wore her hair pulled back in a leather clip. She hadn't said a word about Alma's arm.

"We'll have to start over." Karen began gathering the cards into a pile.

"Forget it," said Jessie. "Do Alma's future."

Alma laughed and stood up. "No, thanks. I've got to water my plants. You girls have fun."

Alma filled her milk jugs and began her work. Whenever her rash started tickling, she splashed water across her skin. Most likely it was a simple case of poison ivy, already past its prime. It wasn't so bad. She ought not to worry.

Five A.M. and Alma couldn't fall back to sleep. In her dream she'd been walking barefoot through a field, and she kept stepping on bees. Her feet were the size of pumpkins.

When she woke, she found Chuck sleeping at the edge of the bed, near the wall and the window. She was completely on the other side.

Her rash was in hysterics. She must have been scraping her arms back and forth over the sheets. She felt tears burning in her eyes. This rash made no sense. Maybe she had leprosy. Or a kind of herpes that prowled her arms and announced itself in bright red, blinking neon. She thought of Jessie's words: "It's one thing to sing the beloved." She felt close to knowing. If she just drifted, maybe the meaning would

emerge in the space between sleep and waking. She closed her eyes . . .
relaxed . . . relaxed . . .

Her tongue felt swollen and liquid in her mouth. The backs of her
eyelids were purple. Something swirled through her mind, and she
summoned her energy, willed her tongue to speak the words that
would be truth.

"Car door," she said.

She sat straight up in bed. Footsteps. Someone was walking in the
hallway. She thought frantically of objects she could use as weapons.
The lamp, a shoe. Then she realized—it must be Jessie.

Alma lay down, then sat up again. Maybe Jessie needed something. Maybe she was sick.

Alma untangled herself from the covers. She opened the bedroom
door and stepped into the hall. Quietly she called out, "Jessie?" She
heard feet shuffling over the carpet, the creak of a step. She couldn't
see anyone. All she could see was the dark form of the bureau halfway
down the hall, just above the stairs.

A whisper. "It's Karen."

Alma had trouble organizing her thoughts. She considered giving
Karen a tidbit of interesting information: the bureau in the hall was
where Alma stored her wigs. She said, "Is everything all right?"

"Yes," said Karen. "Good night."

"Good night," said Alma.

Alma went back into her bedroom and closed the door. She got into
bed and pulled the sheet up. Jessie and Karen.

One evening several years ago, Alma had checked the car's odome-
ter after work—she was watching to see when three thousand miles
passed, then she'd get the oil changed. By chance, she checked again
the next morning and found that fifty-seven miles had been added
overnight. By whom? By Chuck? By one of the kids? Maybe Chuck
had a lover in St. Joseph, maybe one of her sons had driven to a farm
in Kansas and bought a carload of marijuana. Someone had left the

house in the middle of the night and driven fifty-seven miles. She knew she should ask, but she couldn't; she didn't.

Now, lying in bed, Alma couldn't decide: either she would have to ask Jessie to leave, or else it was none of her business.

She turned around and knew nothing, turned and knew nothing, turned, turned, nothing, nothing. And nothing to sing. Sing, thing, beloved.

For days, Alma hid from Jessie, hid from Karen, watered her flowers late at night. Whenever she heard Jessie approaching, Alma put down her book, her dust rag, and walked quickly to another room. Jessie could stay, Alma had decided, but Alma wouldn't make any efforts to be friendly. We're different, Alma thought. We're just too different. Sometimes, as she waited for Jessie and Karen to leave the porch, it got so late Alma didn't water her plants at all. And when she did water them, she couldn't stop thinking about the Guatemalan flower women. The more perfect a bloom, the uglier it seemed, even the flowers that had never been to Guatemala, the ones Alma had tended from seed.

One evening Karen brought homemade tabbouleh in a beautiful blue bowl. She showed Alma the chopped bits of parsley, grown in pots in Karen's own kitchen.

"Why don't you keep that for yourself?" said Alma.

"I made it for you," Karen said, extending her arms.

"I just bought groceries, and I don't have an inch to spare in the fridge. You just keep that for yourself."

One night at supper Alma mentioned selling the house, and Chuck just looked at her. "It's my house," he said. "Why should I?"

One day she got a postcard announcing the new location of Cheryl's shop, now called Pretty Lady. Alma stuck the postcard to her refrigerator with a magnet.

She knew there was a chance that her arm said nothing. And that

seemed like the worst possibility of all. That she might be a flat surface. That someone might touch her and find nothing.

*The words tottered and tiptoed. Beloved: was she? What was it
to be loved?*

Kneeling by the zinnias, some days later, Alma heard the scrape of
Jessie's cane on the sidewalk. She stopped cutting flowers, held still.
At the bottom of the steps, Jessie waited, cocked her head to listen.
Alma saw that she looked agitated; her hair was flying crazily.

"Jessie?" called Alma. "Is everything okay?"

"Can you help me?"

Alma left her scissors on the grass, her basket of flowers.

"What's wrong?"

"I can't find Winston."

The cat. Karen's cat. Alma relaxed a bit. "You think she might have
run away?"

"I don't know. She never has before. Karen just took her to be
spayed, and she wanted me to check in. Karen's in Des Moines until
Thursday. I'm worried."

Karen lived only five blocks away, on Troost, the street that divided
the city into black and white. Alma almost never walked in that direction. The houses were smaller—rentals. The block that Karen lived on
had been marked for demolition, with the land to be used for a research
park someday. Karen lived there month to month, not knowing if she'd
have to move. It was one of the issues Jessie had made a sign for.

"Will you come with me?" Jessie asked.

"Of course," said Alma. "Let's look and see."

"I'll take your arm," said Jessie. "We'll get there quicker." They
walked briskly, bodies close, not saying much. The rash prickled
from the touch of cloth against skin, skin against skin. Alma concentrated on the sidewalk, counted cracks and curbs.

At Karen's house, Jessie pulled a key chain from her skirt pocket and unlocked the door. The living room was hazy bright, with sheer yellow curtains and matted-down shag carpet.

"Any ideas?" asked Alma. It seemed crazy to ask a blind person to watch a cat. What was Karen thinking? Probably the cat had snuck out, gliding right past Jessie.

"Maybe under chairs," said Jessie. "I don't know. I couldn't find her before."

Alma bent and crouched. When she found a penny or a safety pin or a matchbook, she picked it up and put it on a table. She got on her knees to look under the sofa. In the heat of Karen's house, she felt fuzzy headed, disconnected. She heard Jessie bumping around.

Nowhere. Not in the living room. Not in the dining room. She followed a brownish trail, bent to look under Karen's bed, lifted the batik spread, not there. Then as she straightened, she saw the cat, huddled and miserable under a chair. A pool of blood. Moving closer, Alma caught her breath. The stitches had broken loose, and a jumble of intestines had fallen through the opening in its belly.

"What is it?" Jessie asked frantically. "What?"

"Jessie, the cat." Alma tried to speak calmly, but the words crashed and skidded. "The stitches. Where does Karen keep her towels?"

"I don't know. The bathroom. I'll look. I'll get one."

The cat, too weak to move, whimpered as Alma wrapped a bath towel around it, swaddling it, trying to keep the intestines close.

Leaving Jessie with the cat, Alma ran home for the car. She scarcely had time to wonder about the impression she made, gasping for air, a middle-aged woman racing down the sidewalk in muddy, blood-splashed gardening clothes. She had tended her children through stitches and broken bones. She'd been calm then—relatively calm—but now she was out of practice. Poor Karen, thought Alma. Poor girl.

In the car, Jessie stroked the top of the cat's head with one finger and said its name softly, "Winston, pretty Winston."

"She likes that," said Alma.

The skin on Jessie's face was pulled tight. The tendons in her neck showed under the surface. "Alma," she said, "will you tell me exactly what has happened?"

Alma's arms were red and blistered, and she didn't know why; she couldn't think why. The streets she drove through looked unfamiliar, though she knew their names. There were doughnut shops everywhere, and old men in baggy trousers. Alma gripped the wheel hard with both hands. "The stitches must have split apart—oh, Jessie, the cat's insides have fallen out. There was blood in Karen's bedroom. It's all over you, all over the car—I don't mind, that's not why I'm telling you—I'm just telling you so you'll know."

Alma and Jessie followed the vet into the examining room. But as he unwrapped the towel, Alma felt faint, the blood rushing to her feet. She found her way out of the room, and Jessie followed soon after.

In the waiting room, they sat on the vet's sofa. Once Alma regained her equilibrium, she chattered about anything, just to fill the silence. "This is the ugliest room you could imagine. All plaid, the worst colors, avocado, mustard, rust. Do you know what plaid is?"

"Of course," said Jessie.

"The walls are covered with paneling, like somebody's rec room. All around are posters of cats and dogs and rabbits and horses with those cutesy little sayings."

Jessie laughed. "Don't read them. Please."

For a long time they sat in silence. "Jessie," Alma said finally. "I think the cat will die."

"I know."

Jessie's hand moved through the air until it touched Alma's arm. She ran her fingers over the place where the rash grew—the skin raged, roared. It seemed as if Jessie was writing the rash, punching dots into the skin. Alma put her hand on top of Jessie's, and waited.

"It's Rilke," said Jessie.

"I know," said Alma, though she hadn't known, didn't know. All she knew was that the cat was ripped open, and everything was falling out.

"He wrote his poems standing on a rock that overlooked the ocean. The *Duino Elegies*. 'Every angel is terrible.' I don't know what any of it means. I don't think anyone knows."

Alma held on to Jessie's hand. "It's one thing to sing the beloved," she said. The words were still tangled, like a drawer full of necklaces. The rash still crawled across Alma's arm, red and mysterious, itchy and mute.

"I'm sorry," said Jessie.

Alma looked at Jessie, at her thin, fine face, a horse face, a fox face. She thought of all they didn't know.

"In our house," said Alma, "we have a beautiful wooden bureau, and it's full of all my old wigs from when I used to wear wigs. And photo albums. And Christmas tablecloths."

"The cat," said Jessie, "tell me again."

THUNDERATION

I.

ast cartwheels, go!" said Francie.

Francie and Lisa went together, fast and faster across the yard, with their arms and legs straight out and blurring. They rested at the fence, leaning back against the slats, and then I went, turning and turning until I was dizzy. I was halfway across the yard and upside-down when I noticed Joanne sitting on the steps—a swirl of red against the gray porch. There was room for two more cartwheels before the fence, but I caught myself instead and landed heavily, pressing deep ovals into the ground with my toes. The mud felt firm and damp under my feet; the grass was flat and tired.

Joanne had on a floppy red sun hat, a red halter top, and a big, breezy skirt that made me think of gypsies dancing. Her earrings were long and dangly, made of colored beads and bits of metal that flashed silver in the sun. She was twenty-three and beautiful—Francie's big sister. I ran over and sat next to her on the step.

"Hey, Sarah Green-Knees," she said.

I rubbed my hands together, brought them close to my face, and smelled mud and summer. "Ha-ha," I said, and reached out like I was going to touch her. "How about a nice dirt dress?"

"No, but thanks for asking."

"I like your shirt," I said. It had ribbons at the shoulder to hold it up and lots of colored buttons for decoration.

"Thanks. I got it for college." She fluffed her skirt. "I got this whole outfit for college. I'm leaving Sunday."

"I know."

"Are you going to miss me?"

"Of course," I said.

In front of us the Wellings' yard was scattered with dark places, streaks and skids where the grass was pounded down, the green stirred into the brown. Francie and my little sister, Lisa, were still practicing, looking sweaty and serious. Lisa's braids were almost gone, the rubber bands barely hanging on. I could get my hair to last all day, because I braided tight, but Lisa's hair was so straight it slipped out. Francie was in fifth grade, eleven years old, the same as me, but she got her hair cut and styled every three weeks by a beautician named Carlo.

We watched Francie run across the yard diagonally; she jumped with her legs almost in splits, her arms light and airy, out to the sides. Her gymnastics class had a special dancing teacher who showed them how to do arms and fingers like in ballet. Francie showed us some things from her class, but not arms and fingers. You needed special instructions for that, she said; no one would teach it for free.

"She looks good, doesn't she?" Joanne said. We watched some more, and then she called out, "You look like an antelope, Francie."

Francie landed hard on her knees at the end of a jump and turned around. "God, Joanne, shut up."

"I just mean you look graceful."

128

"You're going to make me mess up."

Joanne took a breath in, then pushed it out again, being patient and nice, like always. "I came out to see if you guys wanted to work on the puppets. The heads are baked, and I have more material we can look through."

Lisa ran over to us. "I want to."

"Me, too," I said.

Francie came inside with us without saying anything.

Joanne's puppet supplies—glue, scissors, glitter, and everything— were in the spare bedroom, on the rollaway bed in a big box. Beside the box lay four bald clay heads. These were our second heads. The first ones fell off the baking tray while Joanne was taking them out of the kiln.

Francie rummaged through and picked out the nicest head, the one with the best nose. "I guess they're all the same."

I reached fast for the second-best head.

"We put initials on them," said Lisa.

Francie turned the head over in her hands. "Sorry," she said. "It's yours." She rolled it across the bed to Lisa. The head I had picked up turned out to be the one I had made, but I didn't recognize it. The cheeks were caved in, and the nose was much pointier than I remembered.

Joanne rattled a packet of plastic eyes. "Here's looking at you," she said, then she began pulling pieces of material out of the fabric bag and smoothing them flat. She wanted to be a teacher, and she liked to practice on us. Joanne always had anything we needed for arts and crafts; at my house, with my brothers, you were lucky to find a crayon that someone wasn't chewing on.

Before, when I made my head, I didn't plan a body to go with it, so now I sat thinking, watching Joanne fold the cloth, and waiting for inspiration. Lisa didn't know what to do, either. She liked to think for a long time before she decided anything. To fill the time she got some glue from the box and poured it on her hand. Then she opened a packet of silver glitter and sprinkled the sparkles onto the glue.

"Freckles," said Joanne. She took the glitter from Lisa and sprinkled it around, into the air and on our heads. "O elves, O fairies, O children of the woods," she said.

"Ouch," said Francie. "That got in my eye."

"Sorry." Joanne put the glitter down and went back to folding and unfolding the cloth. After a while she pulled out a scrap I liked—big green-and-yellow flowers splashed wildly onto orange.

"That could be a go-go dancer," I said.

"Hey, good idea," said Joanne. She smiled at me, then turned to Francie to show her a piece of material with red checks. "Why don't you—"

"Don't help us," Francie said, irritated. "Let us do these ourselves."

Lisa looked at Francie, then at Joanne. She blew hard on her hand until the white glue faded and the silver specks looked like they were part of her skin. "I'll use that," she said. "It's pretty."

I was thinking about fringe, figuring out how to cut it, so I didn't even notice when another of Francie's sisters came in the room. I didn't notice her until she dropped the laundry basket on the floor—then I jumped. "Joanne, get this crap out of here," she said. "This room is not for your exclusive use."

Katharine was three years younger than Joanne, and bossy. She scraped the ironing board across the floor and opened it. She ironed a blouse, then pulled her T-shirt over her head. We all watched her.

"That's my bra," said Joanne. "I was looking for that."

"It was in my room," said Katharine.

"No, it wasn't." Joanne's voice rose. "I washed and ironed all my bras and underwear, and you took them. I'm trying to pack, and you're making everything hard for me."

Katharine shook her head in amazement. "You're the only person in the world who would iron a bra." She buttoned the blouse, pulled a pair of pink underwear out of the laundry basket, and left the room.

The whole bed shook when Joanne stood up; the puppet heads rocked between the folds of the bedspread. She ran out the door. "Those are mine," she yelled. "They're *mine!*"

Francie didn't even look up, just kept rolling her clay head around on the bed. I looked at my material, a bright garden of flat flowers, at Francie's bald, ugly puppet head rolling face up, face down across the pillow. I looked at Lisa, then at the door. Our mom would make us clean if we went home, but we had to do it sometime anyway.

"We have to go," I said.

"See you later," said Francie, like we were gone already.

We passed Joanne's room on the way out. She had beads instead of a door, and I saw her through the orange strings. She was sitting on her bed, breathing hard, with her mother next to her. I heard Mrs. Welling say, "Sharing is what families do," in a quiet, controlled voice.

Downstairs, Katharine was on the phone, slapping the cord against the floor like a jump rope, laughing and talking. We walked past her and stepped outside, shutting the door tight, so their air-conditioning would stay in.

"Noisy house," I said, once we were down the block and away. Francie was lucky to have art supplies and glitter and Joanne for a sister, but sometimes her house had too much yelling. "Why do you think they're so mean? It seems like everyone should like Joanne. Doesn't it seem like that?"

Lisa thought for a while. "Maybe it's a habit, like biting fingernails. Maybe they don't notice."

We turned on Brookside and kept walking slowly, the long way, toward dusting and scrubbing and home.

I woke up late that night from the cold and the murmuring, my mother's voice moving quietly above me, at bed level. Hot nights in the summer we all slept on the floor in my parents' room, in the chill and hum of the air-conditioning.

"She asked to borrow the truck, and I told her that I would drive her," said Mom. "She called from a phone booth, crying. I couldn't even tell who it was at first. She says Donna and Larry can't take her until the weekend and can only take what will fit in the car. She's afraid they won't be able to bring everything she needs. It was right before dinner when she called, and I was trying to hold on to the phone, pound the round steak, and watch the boys all at the same time. She wants to be a teacher."

"And teach who?" said Dad. "She's not stable. Tell me who in the world would hire her?"

"I know. Poor girl. She's so nervous I worry about her. I can't picture her actually sitting down to study."

"She doesn't act like a person who should go to college. She acts like she's nuts."

"We do have the truck," Mom said. "It won't hurt to help her out. It's her big dream. We'll load her up and go."

They stopped talking, but I couldn't sleep. I just had a sheet over me, and I was cold. I was tired, but I couldn't fall asleep. Joanne would be better than a lot of teachers I had. Why wouldn't she? She liked kids. She liked us. I rolled around restlessly, and eventually bumped into Lisa, but she didn't wake up. I couldn't figure anything out. It was too dark to think. I wished I was sleeping somewhere else. I wished I was in a bed, instead of lying on a hard floor, freezing and wide awake.

The next morning, early, Joanne banged on our door, then came into the kitchen without waiting. We were still eating breakfast. "Are you ready?" she said, excited and out of breath. Her eyes looked at all of us and everywhere.

"Slow down," said Mom. "Sit down. First one thing, then the next." She told Joanne to feed Matt, then went to get ready.

Joanne rattled the spoon into the little jar, metal against glass. She spilled the first spoonful onto the high-chair tray. I saw that her hands were shaking. Matt started to cry.

I said, "Hi, baby," and grabbed his hand before he could smear the food around.

"You do it, Sarah," said Joanne. She gave the spoon to me and sat straight in the chair, smiling and waiting.

When we got to the Wellings' house, Lisa and I carried boxes from Joanne's room to our truck. The beads were gone from her doorway, so you didn't drift and weave into her room anymore; you walked straight in and straight out. The smells were gone, too, the grape candles and dried flowers all packed away. The room smelled like nothing, like carpet and paint.

Katharine watched us carrying everything. When I walked past, she shook her head like she couldn't believe it, and I felt embarrassed. Every time Joanne walked past, Katharine said something. "People don't bring their whole lives to college," she said. "You don't even realize that dorm rooms are small. You think college is going to be some big rah-rah place. You're not being realistic at all." Francie wasn't there to say good-bye; she had diving first and then a haircut, and Mrs. Welling was driving Francie around. Mr. Welling was at work.

We were crowded in the truck, and Joanne talked the whole way. "When I'm a teacher," she said, "I'll do a different bulletin board every week. Maybe I'll do practice bulletin boards for my bedroom—autumn leaves, Valentine's Day, It's a Small World After All. I have a lot of ideas."

"I'm sure you'll be a very dedicated teacher," said Mom.

When we got to Lawrence, we had to carry everything to the third floor of the place where she was staying, some kind of house where girls lived. Inside there was a beauty parlor hair dryer—the kind old ladies sit under—on the landing. It was aqua colored with a wide plastic seat. We made hundreds of trips up and down, and every time I got to the landing I looked at the hair dryer and thought about sitting down.

Joanne's new roommate stood near the window and watched us moving everything.

"That's a good idea," said Joanne. "Having a hair dryer here."

The girl looked at her, surprised. "No one uses it really. It's just for a joke."

"Oh." Joanne kept looking at me like I was supposed to do something. I searched for a place to set my box. "So I guess that's everything. This is Sarah and Lisa, by the way."

"Your sisters?"

"No," said Joanne. "Friends of mine. Oh, and by the way, I have an ironing board and a steam iron if you ever want to use them."

"I do, too," said the girl.

"Records, popcorn maker, lots of candles, magazines, different things."

The girl nodded, but didn't look interested.

"I'm hoping we'll be good friends," said Joanne.

"Sure, me, too." The girl looked at her watch. "Oops, it's lunchtime," she said. "See you later."

The box I was holding was full of puppet supplies, and whenever I shifted the box, the packet of plastic eyes bobbled around and looked in different directions. Joanne had boxes and boxes of things you would put on a dresser: piggy banks, teacups, Beatles statues with bouncing heads. The puppet box was heavy, and my arms were tired. Finally I found a tiny empty space, and I put the box there.

Lisa, Joanne, and I stood in the middle of all her boxes. "My dad said he would throw away anything I left," said Joanne. "He says he's not a warehouse." She kept turning around in the middle of everything. "Do you need any candles?"

"No," I said. "We have enough."

"I better say good-bye to your mom," she said.

Mom was waiting at the truck. She hugged Joanne and said,

"Good luck." Then Lisa hugged Joanne, and then I did. "You'll remember me, won't you?" she said, laughing a little and still hugging my head.

"We'll miss you," said Lisa.

"We'll write you letters," I said.

We got in the truck and watched until she got to the front door. She stopped. She looked like she was waiting to cross a street with too many cars and no stoplight. She picked a piece of ivy off the railing, and I could see the leaf fluttering in her hand.

"Don't worry about your roommate," I said. "She's stupid." But she didn't hear; she smiled and waved and walked inside.

"Poor girl," said Mom.

Without Joanne, there was plenty of room in the truck, but I moved over, close to Mom, and Lisa sat so her leg was touching mine. I thought about what I would write in a letter. I wished we had given Joanne a picture of us. She would remember Francie automatically, but she could easily forget about Lisa and me.

For three weeks after Joanne left, everything was hot and boring. It was the worst part of summer. We still had ten days before school, and Francie was always busy, at lessons or getting new clothes for school. Mom said, "I can keep you busy," but she meant changing diapers and washing windows.

The pool still wouldn't open. At the beginning of the summer, Lisa and I had gone every day to see when it would open, but now we only went sometimes, when we felt hot and mad.

We stood outside now, looking through the fence at tires and beer cans in dirty water.

"Remember how pretty the pool looked with snow in it?" Lisa said.

"No." I threw a stick past the bars of the gate.

We walked back past Beauty Unlimited, past church and school, past Jake's Barbecue. "Stupid pool," I said, feeling like I had been tricked into hoping for the whole summer.

"We could go home and take baths."

"Yippee," I said.

"We could wash our hair in buckets in the backyard."

When Lisa was little, she got in trouble at school for bringing dreams to show and tell, instead of a doll or a bracelet. If you looked at her now, scuffing her feet along the sidewalk, you would think she was just a regular girl. But she wasn't.

"With rainwater," she said. "It's better than being hot and doing nothing."

When we got to Francie's block, I turned and Lisa followed me. We went to the back of the house first, into the shaggy backyard.

We walked on the path—half dirt, half cement—on the side of their house, stepping softly so we could scare Francie if she was there. I heard something, a wild rustling noise, like animals playing in trash. Or like someone wrapping presents with stiff, loud paper. "What is that?" I whispered.

We looked through the fence, through the wild roses and bare green lilac bushes, past fat tomatoes held up by sticks and panty hose, and we saw the noise—Joanne, with pompons, cheerleading.

She was staring straight ahead, singing in a voice as soft as a trance. "Thunder, thunderation, we're the Bobcat delegation, when we fight with determination, we create a sensation." On the word "sen-sa-tion" Joanne shook the tissue paper pompons in front of her with slow-motion punches. She pronounced each word like it was a secret password that she was trying to remember forever.

"She's cheerleading," whispered Lisa.

I nodded. "I know." Joanne had been a cheerleader at her junior college the year before. Once Lisa, Francie, and I went to a game with her, but it rained, and she was the only cheerleader there. She didn't really cheer; mostly she yelled things like, "Go!" and "All right, you guys!" Then after the game, her car wouldn't start, and she was crying, with her head down on the steering wheel. Mom had to come get us in the station wagon, with Robert, Brian, and William buckled in the back and Matt in the car seat.

Joanne didn't see us or hear us. Her eyes were focused tight and far away, concentrating hard enough to set a stick on fire. There didn't seem to be enough room, or air, back there for so much concentration. The backyard was as humid as our cellar in the summer, and tense, and I thought of a jar we found down there once, badly canned with the steel lid swelling. The jar seemed about to burst into glass and sauce and skinned tomatoes.

Lisa put her hand on her forehead and wiped sweat away. "Let's go," she whispered.

I turned to go but was distracted by the roses near my face—red flowers side by side with dead ones. I wanted to stay, to watch Joanne sing and to smell the sick-sweetness, but I forced myself to turn instead, and I followed Lisa down the path.

We walked to the front and knocked on the door. Katharine answered. "Francie's at diving," she said. I wanted to ask why Joanne was home and when she was leaving and what she was doing, but Katharine closed the door—because of the air-conditioning—before I could ask anything.

"Oh, I forgot. Wednesday. Diving." I spoke to Lisa and to the front door. We walked away.

"Maybe she came home to wash her dirty clothes," I said.

"She's here, but she didn't call us." Lisa spoke slowly. "It's strange that she didn't call us."

"Maybe she came home to get something she forgot."

"Maybe she tried to call, and we were gone."

When we got home, Lisa hooked up the sprinkler, but the hose had been in the sun, and the water came out boiling hot at first, then lukewarm, like used bathwater. I pictured Francie diving into cool water at their club pool, playing Marco Polo, drinking a Coke with a thousand ice cubes.

I watched rusty water drops run down my leg in crazy patterns, felt warm water in my hair and on my back.

I went inside to call Joanne, but she couldn't talk, Katharine said. Francie was at diving.

*L*isa called Joanne the next day and we went over. We stood in the Wellings' living room, Lisa and I facing Francie and Joanne across the coffee table. Joanne looked tired, like she had been awake for a long time. Francie looked embarrassed.

Lisa gave Joanne a candle that looked like a Hershey's Kiss. It was supposed to smell like chocolate when you lit it.

"Sorry about college," I said. "That's too bad."

"Let's not dwell on it," said Joanne. "Now I can be with you guys more. We should do something fun, like a show. A special show with tumbling. Puppets." Joanne sat down at the piano. "We can sing." She shuffled through a stack of sheet music. "Here's a good song," she said. "It's a round." She sang, " 'C-O-F-F-E-E. Coffee is not for me. It's a drink you can wake up with. That it makes you nervous is no myth. Slave to a coffee cup, I can't give coffee up.' "

"We hate coffee," said Francie.

Joanne played another song called "Under the Umbrella of the Red, White, and Blue, America, America, Our Hats Off to You," but Francie hated that song, too. "It's not the Fourth of July," she said.

Joanne didn't say anything. She put her hand up to the metronome on the lid of the piano, turned it on to slow, and watched it ticking. Her black hair was long and frizzy across her back.

Lisa tapped her on the shoulder and said, "Joanne?"

"Don't bother," said Francie. She stomped out of the room, but you couldn't hear any noise because of the carpet. She flung the front door open and acted like she was going to slam it, then didn't. She just closed it instead.

"I don't like coffee," I said to Joanne. "But I liked that song. I liked both of the songs."

"Yeah," said Lisa. "I like songs that are rounds. And songs about America."

"Francie's just being unpleasant," I said. I couldn't tell if Joanne was listening or not, but I decided to sing anyway, to try and make her feel better. " 'This land is your land, this land is my land, from California to the New York Islands.' " Lisa started to sing, too. I thought Joanne would sing or play the piano, but she didn't. She kept staring straight ahead, at the metal arm making small slices in the air. She wasn't listening. We could have clapped in her ear, and she wouldn't have noticed.

We stopped singing then and left. We went across the carpet, out the door, and outside.

"What are we supposed to do?" I asked.

Francie was sitting on the porch with her knees hugged into her chest. When I sat beside her, she stood up without looking at me and walked into the yard. She dropped onto her knees and did a chest roll, then another, then another, lurching forward each time, arching so that she pressed into the ground: stomach, chest, neck, chin, and over. They were her favorite thing to do. At our class picnic in May, she did twenty—showing off—in the thick grass of an unmowed hill.

Now she pushed herself into a standing position, and I saw that her shirt was muddy. She wobbled and took small, dizzy steps like she was learning to walk.

"Did Joanne get kicked out of college?" I asked.

Francie didn't look up. She acted like she didn't hear me. Finally she said, "If we're doing a show, we definitely need to have chest rolls. That's decided."

"I hate chest rolls," I said. Their yard had slugs, and I didn't like the thought of my face smashing into one. I didn't want to think about a tumbling routine when Joanne was so sad.

"They demonstrate flexibility," she said. "In competition they're Class Two difficulty."

"So what? Number one, they're ugly. Number two, they hurt."

"What you mean to say is that you can't do them," she said, nodding slowly. "I understand."

"I *know how* to do them. I don't *want to*."

"Then I'll have to do a solo." All I could hear in her voice was meanness. Once my mother said that Francie was a fair-weather friend and that I should make other friends. Francie looked at me with a snobby smile, then flipped over into a front walkover. But it wasn't very graceful because when her feet hit the ground, she farted.

Lisa giggled a little, but I laughed loud and mean. I was as mean as Francie.

"Shut up," she said. Her face got red, from being embarrassed and from being upside down. "It's not funny, it's natural. Don't be a jerk, Sarah." She stood up like she was going to go into her house.

"Okay," I said. "I'm sorry."

"I think chest rolls would be nice," Lisa said.

So we put them all over the routine, and Francie had a solo of five in a row. If a hunter had come to the yard looking for animal prints, he would have wondered about all the chin marks in the mud.

When Joanne came out, her hair was under control, tight in a bun. But her voice was dull, and slow as the metronome. "What are you doing?" she said. "That can't be good for your necks."

"I know," I said. "They're detrimental."

"Don't you care about your spines?"

"I do," I said. "I care about my spine."

"We *love* our spines," said Francie.

"I better take you guys to get ice cream before you're paralyzed. While you can still hold your own cones."

"I'm not hungry," said Francie.

Joanne went inside to get money, and Lisa and I got into her old yellow Volkswagen, me in front, Lisa in back. "I think she feels better," said Lisa. "She seems peppier."

"Let's hope so," I said.

Joanne's car was a mess, boxes and junk all over. Lisa had to put her feet inside a box. I put mine on the ladybug floor mat.

When Joanne came out with her big, red purse, Francie was trailing right behind. She slipped in back and sat next to Lisa, quiet.

At the ice cream store, Lisa, Francie, and I got bubblegum; Joanne got mocha. We sat in pink plastic chairs by the windows and ate without talking. I watched as the store got crowded, people milling and shoving. The employees were working frantically behind the counter.

Joanne stood up suddenly and made her way to the counter, squeezing through all the people.

"Where's she going?" said Lisa.

We were all watching. Joanne said something to a girl who was scooping ice cream, and the girl looked confused. She walked slowly to where brown aprons were hanging on a hook. She took an apron and handed it to Joanne.

Francie shook her head very slowly.

"What did she do?" I said. "Ask for a job?"

Francie made a sound like a moan. Lisa and I sat watching. Joanne put on a hat and stepped behind the counter. We were through with our ice cream, so we played with our napkins and our pink spoons, and we looked at the people crowding around. Joanne looked determined and serious as she scooped. She handed people their ice cream without smiling.

"She's like a robot," said Lisa.

"She's sick," Francie said flatly, eyes straight ahead. "That's the whole problem."

"She shouldn't do that if she's sick," I said. "She'll give people germs."

"She's not contagious," said Francie.

"Then what is she?"

"She's just Joanne," said Lisa.

Francie stared and said nothing. I looked at the ceiling fan and watched the blades whirl and blur. "What is she?" I said.

"She gets depressed," Francie said finally. "She has to take medicine. It's not her fault, she can't help it. Someone called from her college and said to come get her. College was too hard and she felt lonesome."

Francie wouldn't look at me. "The first time anyone knew she was sick was when she was in high school. She was afraid to go to school, and she had to stay in the hospital. I remember once I went there with my mother, and Joanne was crying, so I cried, too. I was just a little kid. Sometimes I would go in her room at home and pretend the stuffed animals were Joanne." She stopped. "You can't tell anyone at school," she said.

"Why would I? It's not true."

"Just don't."

"You're the one who would tell people."

We sat without looking at each other. Joanne looked frazzled and held the ice cream scooper high and ready.

We waited and waited for Joanne to finish, but she kept scooping. The girl who gave her the apron finished her shift and left, and other workers came out of the back and put on hats and clean aprons.

I went up to the counter. "May I help you?" said Joanne.

"It's me," I said.

She looked at me. "Sarah."

I felt people crowding all around me. Someone stepped on my foot, and when I looked down, I saw a flat leather sandal, but no leg. "Ouch," I said. I put my arm up high, reaching for her like I was in deep water.

"I've got to get this line down to size," she said.

"Is this your job?"

"I'm helping out," she said. She stared over my head into the crowd. "See all the people?"

I didn't look at the people; I looked at her. The front of her apron was soaked with melted ice cream, mostly chocolate. Her arms were splotched with different colors, like a terrible disease.

A tanned, wrinkled woman in a white tennis dress bumped me, and I felt her polyester scratching on my arm. "Daiquiri ice," she said to Joanne, and Joanne bent down into the freezer. Through the smeared glass I could see her arm circling around and around inside the ice cream bucket. I knocked on the glass. "We're going to be late for dinner," I said, but she didn't look up. "I have to set the table. We have to go." She was rounding the ice cream into a ball, patting it with the scooper.

"We have to get home," I said, raising my voice. I was almost shouting.

Over at the line of pink chairs, Lisa was swinging her legs, tapping on her teeth with her pink spoon. Francie looked sad, and I felt sad with her. More and more people were crowding through the door, pushing forward, pressing me against the glass. Joanne looked past me, not seeing me, and I felt panicky and not old enough. Her arm darted above the counter, and I grabbed at the silver flash of the scooper. "You have to bring us home," I said. "You brought us here."

"Sugar cone?" said Joanne.

II.

Nine years later I am twenty, and listening to the background music at Joanne's wake: Marvin Gaye singing "I Heard It through the Grapevine" and "Sexual Healing." He's dead, too. The lid on the coffin is down. Four days ago Joanne swallowed a bottle of sleeping pills and some water, then passed out on her parents' sofa. Home from college for the summer, sitting in a chair on the front porch of my parents' house, I heard the sirens the next block over. Joanne spent two days in the hospital, conscious and semiconscious, and sorry, telling everyone that she'd made a mistake, that she didn't know what she was doing. But by the time she realized she wanted to live, she died anyway.

Joanne's high school senior picture is propped up against the gleaming wood, and she smiles, though that was the year that took her three years to finally finish, with the interruptions and depressions and hospitals. That picture was the most recent one the Wellings had, except for a blurry Polaroid, in which she wears red and beads and bits of sparkle, and stands beside a tree.

Lisa and I wear dark, plain dresses and hold purses. Francie is tall and tanned; she's on the swim team at her college. In Joanne's honor, she wears bangles, spangles, fringe, and beads. The other sisters wear gaudy thrift store hats, Joanne's hats; they hug and cry. The day before the accident, Joanne asked her sisters, did anyone want to go see the free concert at Brush Creek, take a picnic and a Frisbee? No one wanted to. She called our house, and I said no; Lisa said no; my mom said no. This is what we all think about, wonder about, this chorus of no's.

The funeral director glides through the crowd. He unfolds chairs so gently that it seems he is smoothing them open. People sink into the velvet cushions, draw rosaries from pockets and purses. I can hear the click of beads, feeble and jittery, under the louder sounds of talk and crying. Across the room Francie's earrings glitter, and I watch them; I want them.

One evening when I was younger, Joanne took Lisa and me to Penn Valley Community College to her elementary education class. For her final project, she'd coached us in a children's play, and now we were going to perform it for her class. We were snakes and our job was to hiss and slither while Joanne narrated a story about St. Patrick driving the snakes out of Ireland.

In the bathroom at the college, we changed into green tights and green leotards. As we were dressing, Joanne rushed out to check on the sets, the costumes, the scripts, something. "Just wait," she said. "I'll be back."

Lisa and I bundled our clothes and shoes, played with the hand dryers, twirled the knobs on the sanitary napkin machine, and then waited near the bathrooms, in a nook carved out for vending machines. We spent our telephone quarters on 7Up, watching the machine drop down a cup, then ice, then a gush of soda. We marveled at another machine that dispensed lunches: ham and cheese sandwiches, apples, yogurt, beef stew in cans. We took turns pressing the button, watching the food rotate. "I think I would like a lemon yogurt," said Lisa. "I think I'll have an apple, please. No, make that an orange."

We waited. We sat on a green vinyl sofa in the lounge area, leaned our heads back and looked up at the square lights that were set into the ceiling. I could see the outlines of moths that had gotten caught under the glass, heaps and piles of moths.

The hallway just beyond our niche was dimly lit, deserted. We stood in our green tights, holding our shoes, slithering, sliding, our feet smooth on the speckled tile. We spun pirouettes on the bottoms of our feet. We waited and waited, but she never did come back.

I am not a stage mother, but I know the value of dreams, even unattainable ones. After Santa Claus, there is another available mythology called Hollywood, which I support by reading *People*. How could I debunk Hollywood? Why should I? Hollywood is shiny and hopeful and bigger than me.

So I didn't mind waking in the sixes this morning, a Saturday, and driving four soft-singing, seat-kicking girls and one overburdened baby to Starlight Theater for the *Little Orphan Annie* auditions. We tiptoed past my husband, Danny, deep asleep on the sagging couch, and then onto the porch, where I stood last night with a past love, close enough to kiss.

We stepped—the girls and I—into a morning dim and dewy with possibility. How could I mind? When I was fourteen and in the chorus of a warm-weather Parks and Rec production of *The Mikado,* my own mother drove me to every rehearsal, every performance, and sat reading and crocheting without complaint.

My Annies are unappreciative of my efforts, even though I packed a lunch that features chocolate cupcakes sealed in plastic and fruit drink in cardboard boxes, straws attached. My girls can't tap-dance, and they hold me responsible, even Adrianne who is a baby and generally forgiving.

The girls do not all belong to me, although in the ordinary day-to-day they each and every call me Mom. Elizabeth and Adrianne are mine; both are dark and charming, like Danny, who is Italian, Scottish, and Cherokee. The other girls—Sunny, Dawn, and Debby—are foster children, probably temporary, although Debby has been with us for three years, and we will keep her if we can. Dawn and Sunny are sisters, ages seven and eight, with a dead father and a mother in Glendale, California, who reminds me, in various ways, of me. Sunny, the older sister, spends hours in the bathroom, trying to curl her meek, straight hair. Dawn has a Mohawk, which will almost certainly limit her chances at stage orphandom, despite the fact that she is practically the genuine article. They arrived two months ago with small, flowered suitcases, and so far, I like them.

At odd intervals throughout the morning, the choreographer has directed the auditioners to skip clockwise around the stage. Before it seemed only a means of crowd control, but now the choreographer wants skipping and smiling, simultaneously. Now it's the real thing. "It's your birthday!" she says, hands clasped in ecstasy. "A clown is coming to do magic tricks at your party, and you are skipping to the door to let him in!" The choreographer, in black tights and a pink cardigan, looks about my age, which is twenty-four. If we went to the same high school, she is no one I remember.

My girls skip bitterly, and badly. At home in the backyard, they giggle and hold carnivals and try to swing over the top bar of the swing set. I could never have predicted that in public they would move so self-consciously. A thousand girls go by, all talented skippers, then Debby, Sunny, Dawn, and Elizabeth, who shout at me as they pass:

"You made us take karate!"

"I *suggested* karate," I say. "I *made* you take tumbling." I don't
have to shout because I have the facts. For the general life of a girl,
cartwheels are always more marketable than shuffle-ball-changes.
"My mother made me take water ballet," I say. "I had to wear a nose
plug and put Jell-O in my hair." But they are gone, swallowed with
a gulp by the skipping stampede. Beside me in the wings, Adrianne
grips a pink plastic bottle, its nipple gummy from the heat. This
morning I dressed her in a tie-dyed baby T-shirt, a Danny original.
It's hard to make such small circles without blurring the design, but
Danny is good with children and details.

After three times around the stage, the choreographer signals (clapping) for the girls to stop, and they bunch up in a far corner of the
stage, panting. The choreographer tells them something that I can't
hear. Maybe she retracts the clown. Maybe she tells them that when
the time comes, tampons are more comfortable than pads. Since I can't
hear, I don't know.

And so I sit cross-legged on the stage and think of a long blue satin
dress that I wore in a high school talent show. I sang "Goodbye, Yellow Brick Road," and my mother accompanied me on the piano,
wearing heavy brown shoes and a dress she didn't like. My father and
his new wife were in the audience, but my mother didn't miss a note.
She began her adult life as a nun and has always been capable of de-
tachment. Certain things she didn't mention then or since, such as: my
voice is only slightly better than ordinary, and my nose and teeth are
not conducive to fame. She wanted me to go to college all along but
didn't press.

At eighteen, when I called her from a gas station to tell her I was
pregnant, she said nothing for a minute or two. Then she said: "Con-
gratulations." She said: "What will you do?" She said: "Darn you for
making me a grandmother before the age of forty."

Danny and I made the best of things; we lived at Ye Olde English
Village Apartments on money from the government and my father,
and we didn't marry until after Elizabeth was born. I visited high

schools in maternity clothes and told classes of freshmen about birth control and how I wished things had happened differently.

The girls are somewhere among the short, anxious, breastless crowd, milling and fretting and practicing "Tomorrow." I have tried to be encouraging, yet realistic. In the car I said, "What you deserve doesn't always happen. This is sometimes good and sometimes bad." I believe this and depend upon it, gladly passing up a few honors to avoid a like number of recriminations.

True: I did not buy orange wigs or permit the girls to dye their hair. The show comes with a traveling Annie from New York. It said in the paper that she's not a natural redhead but moves from city to city with seven wigs on seven Styrofoam heads. The auditions today are to cast twenty local girls as orphans. But each of my Annies is convinced that she can outsing and outdance this outside Annie. They don't really want to be orphans. For the record, I found a nice red outfit for everyone, slacks or a dress, although I am sure that raggedy orphan clothes would be better received by the judges. These red clothes are in addition to tap shoes, a great expense and not likely to get much future use. (Again true: apart from various foot stamping in the cereal section of the grocery store, not one of my Annies has had any practice in the art form of tap-dancing. They *can* do cartwheels, including one-arms, and somersaults—front, back, and straddle.)

Still, I sense bitterness between us, myself and the girls, and now the late-morning sun is overheating my small square of stage. I lotion Adrianne and move her car seat out of the glare, behind dark green curtain folds. Sometimes we call her Sweetpea because she looks like Popeye's baby. She looks at me through one eye, so long and steadily that I am the one who finally breaks the gaze. She is an anxious baby and burps more often than seems necessary. When she gets teeth, I think she will bite her nails. Now she fights sleep for a moment, her lids sinking and straining. I am tired too, out late last night with girlfriends, and she almost takes me with her, into sleep. But there is an electrical outlet near us and a line of mothers holding hot roller sets and noisily debating black ballet slippers versus pink. If I don't take responsibility for my baby's pleasant dreams, who will?

"Ssh," I say.

The mothers glower at me. One says, "Ssh, yourself." Another, holding a purple curling iron (but not in a threatening way) says, "Either she'll sleep or she won't." Which I know is true. And when I peep back at Adrianne, her eyelids seem weighted; she breathes heavily, fast asleep. I flex my sandaled feet and do my best to relax.

Here among the hopefuls, red curls all around me, I can't help but think of Chris Kelly. He surfaces out of swampy high school memories, starts wading through gray matter to the foreground of my brain. His feet are bigger than I remember, and, unfamiliar with the territory as he is, he displaces a few phone numbers.

As I listen to the sloshing of my first boyfriend, two girls, twins or sisters, aged nine or ten, center themselves before me and begin to tapdance. They are competent and earnest but heavy on their feet.

"Land a little softer," I suggest. "Think of cornflakes or snow." They nod, land softer. I'm blond and wearing sunglasses and apparently they think I'm a talent scout. When they finish, they smile at me and wait to be hired. "I'm a mother," I say, lifting the curtain to reveal Adrianne. "It's not up to me."

Disappointment makes them temporarily older, sixteen or seventeen, at least. They stare at me, then dance away without a backward glance, their orange hair bouncing like bedsprings. I peek inside my head and find Chris Kelly, still there. His hair, that gorgeous mop, is more brown than Annie red, but both colors are significantly involved. I'm not exactly sure what to do with him. What will we talk about after so many (seven) years? I owe him certain things, including a fifteen-pound weight loss (welcomed) from mono. One Valentine's Day he gave me two sweaters and twelve pink roses. When we dated, I felt sensual and beautiful (except, of course, during mono). I actually *became* sensual and beautiful—so much so that when I glanced one day at the glamorous baker at the restaurant where Chris and I both worked, the baker—Danny—dropped a glass measuring cup on the floor. Danny told me later that I looked, suddenly, different to him.

Danny: flour in his hair, sweeping glass off the tiles, he was astonishingly handsome then. He is astonishingly handsome now. Women I know, even close friends, have confessed to me feelings of desire. I am still amazed to find myself in the same room with him, much less the same marriage.

Other times it is not so hard to believe.

Chris Kelly shakes his curly hair out of his eyes. He smiles at me, and I smile back. I cannot remember much of what we did together or talked about. Mostly I remember cars and couches, kissing. I remember sitting on metal counters in the restaurant's dish room at the end of the night. Since I remember so little, I invent other memories—a camping trip to Mexico, a lobster dinner before the prom, strawberries and constellations and clean-smelling hair.

We are holding hands when I hear the tap shoes. When I look up, I see that I'm surrounded by grim-faced girls. Chris Kelly squeezes my hand once and steps, discreetly, behind the curtain. "Is it lunchtime yet?" I say, wiping my moist palms. "Are you thirsty?" I offer cardboard rectangles of fruit punch.

Elizabeth (she is five) takes a sip, then pulls the straw out and squirts red liquid onto the wood floor.

"Elizabeth!" I wrench the box upright.

"I don't blame her," says Debby.

I point toward a rusty water fountain overgrown with ivy. "Do you want sandwiches?"

The girls shake their heads, sullenly.

"What's wrong?"

I look at Dawn. The bristles on her Mohawk tremble, and her shaved scalp twitches in spots. This is a strange effect and disconcerting, but lower down her face is sad, her tears authentic. She wails, "We're terrible at dancing."

It's my fault. I'm the one who found the audition ad in the newspaper. I bought the record. At home we practiced leaps across the living room, but I didn't know what I was doing any more than they did. The competition here is ferocious. All around us are girls who own multiple pairs of tights, girls who can sing and dance and probably even ice-skate, girls who have spent entire Saturdays pointing their toes.

The curl has seeped out of Sunny's hair, which falls in front of her face in straight lines. "Nothing is fair," she says.

Elizabeth and Debby look drained and downtrodden, as if they have been tap-danced upon.

The girls stand stiffly around me, and I watch the tears wash down Dawn's face. But what comfort can I give now that Chris Kelly has stepped out of the shadows, naked? Furtively we slide away. It is night, and we are skinny-dipping in a warm, lake-smelling lake. I am forgetting certain things. I breaststroke and feel my hair float like seaweed. The tap shoes make distant, rattling sounds, like stars falling to earth. I'm warm and peaceful. And then suddenly something, someone, gives my hair a tremendous yank.

I hear this: "Who was that man last night?" It is Debby.

"Man?" I say.

"You know," says Elizabeth.

"You mean Daddy?"

"Not *Daddy,*" says Debby. "*He* was working." Danny works at McGillicutty's, where he is a certified chef. It's a good job, with benefits. On Friday nights he works late, past two sometimes, preparing the kitchen for the next day. I imagine him. He tests toasters, organizes the eggs. He drinks a beer and another beer and another beer.

The girls circle around me. The sound of their tap shoes on the wooden floor has an undertone of menace. I feel a chill. I have lifted myself out of the water and onto the dock.

Debby is twelve but responsible. When I go out, she puts the others and herself to bed. I depend upon her. Responsible, relentless, she says, "Who was it? Who was that on our porch?"

So here it is: Chris Kelly is muddying his basketball shoes in my brain right now for a couple of reasons, one being his Annie red and curly hair. The other and more likely reason: I saw him last night when I was out with my girlfriends. He is twenty-one to my twenty-four, in his last year of college, a fraternity member and almost an engineer. (I'll admit that our dating ages—his fourteen to my seventeen—seem unseemly to me now. But Chris was mature for his age, and I was not.) Last night he wore a pink shirt with iron marks and a corduroy jacket, and while my married and unmarried friends sat on the laps of married and unmarried men, we said hello and other things.

"There are things you can't possibly understand," I say.

Chris Kelly did follow me home. There have been a number of bump-and-robs in the city, and our neighborhood is not a good one. He walked up to the door with me, before 1:00 A.M., just like in high school. But he did not step inside.

Debby won't look at my eyes. The girls, like everyone else, love Danny. Who can resist that movie-star smile? He is without a doubt a better cook than me, and on nights when he is the last to leave work, he snags a cheesecake and we eat it at breakfast.

I don't want to cause disloyalties, but there are certain realities.

Debby says, "Where is Sweetpea?"

I point to the curtain, and she ruffles through the material until she finds the baby.

This morning we tiptoed past Danny, across a floor littered with beer cans. He will wake in a bad humor at four or five o'clock. On Saturdays (and Sundays) I like activities that will keep us all out of the house.

Debby emerges from behind the curtain, Adrianne riding on her hip. I begin to hand out sandwiches, but although I have been carefully guarding this backpack of food all morning, the tuna is oozing onto the baggies, and the bread has dissolved.

"Squished!" says Sunny. She holds the messy sandwich at arm's length. "When Danny makes sandwiches, they're never squished."

"Then eat Danny's sandwiches," I say.

"He didn't make any," says Sunny.

I say, "Well, well."

Adrianne is the only one not offended by my food, the only one to offer support. She grabs at Debby's sandwich, puts her hand right in it. She smiles at me. Adrianne was conceived to save a failing marriage, and she takes her job seriously. I feel only partial gratitude, watching her smear tuna in her hair.

We are tired of being here, weary of skipping and waiting and tap-dancing. But we stay. The pink-sweatered choreographer announces "a special treat!" The Annie from New York walks across the stage. The thousand girls murmur. The Annie has a bubbling laugh, in-credible poise. She sings beautifully. First Dawn cries, then Sunny, then Debby, then Elizabeth. I would like to cry myself. Adrianne reaches out and pats my head with her tuna hand. The New York An-nie's voice projects through the theater and beyond, resonating with every emotion. Love, despair, anger, hunger. I hear a strain (no, more—a vein) of sexuality pulsing through. It said in the paper that she is thirteen and binds her breasts with Ace bandages.

"Look," I say, "her wig is crooked."

I can't say that I haven't thought of other highways. If Chris Kelly had asked me last night to go with him somewhere, anywhere, I can't say absolutely that I wouldn't have gone. He didn't ask. The truth is that we don't have much in common. I have become, somehow, a mother of five, a dutiful accompanist. I sit at the piano in heavy brown shoes.

I'm not saying it's hopeless. My mother went back to herself, to age twenty, to a prayer farm in Kansas. But she has made a few adjust-ments in the meanwhile, such as, her tubes are tied.

The girls take off their tap shoes and listen with faces full of enchantment and despair. I will never find Chris Kelly asleep on my couch, surrounded by empties. I will never find him in the kitchen, fine-chopping vegetables. Chris Kelly would never (I am certain) make me egg rolls. But Danny, well, I still like the looks of him.

Driving over here this morning, none of us could remember for sure how the Annie movie ends. Annie, of course, gets adopted, but what about the other orphans? We remembered, vaguely, a scene involving fireworks and cake and new dresses. This morning I asked, "Is it a happy ending if they just get new dresses?" We all decided no.

PORK CHOPS

Gina was standing right beside the boxes she'd piled in the breakfast nook, but neither she nor Phil mentioned them. She knew Phil was worried, but he needn't be. Yes, she was going to move out, but as Gina had said again and again, it was an experiment. It didn't have to be an ending.

She held the Styrofoam meat tray, the six, small, premium pork chops, carefully arranged in two rows of three. Affixed to the clear plastic wrap was a bright orange sticker that said Corn-fed. She pushed a finger into the plastic, then studied the dent in the pinkish grayish flesh. "They're not ours," said Gina. "It's like stealing."

But Phil was already paging through his cookbooks, looking for recipes: pork roast, Chinese pork, pineapple pork. He explained again, patiently: "I went to the store. I picked out my groceries. I waited in line. I paid my money. It's not like I put the pork chops in my pocket or shoved them down the front of my pants, but somehow it happened—they got in my bag. My position"—he laid his hand on his chest for emphasis—"is that if the store screws up, the store should suffer." It was true that he'd noticed the package while he was still in the parking lot at the grocery store, but he was in a hurry then, with barely enough time to get to the dry cleaners before it closed. In any event, he wasn't sorry, and he didn't feel guilty either. He and Gina had come home from the supermarket plenty of times minus some item they'd paid for: dental floss, garlic, laundry soap. Gina was forgetting that, thought Phil. She was forgetting all those other times.

Looking at the pork chops, Gina remembered the foul-smelling petting zoo her parents had taken her to when she was a child, the goats balancing on the fence and bleating, the dank barn and the enormous pig she'd seen there, the ten or twelve snorting, squirming piglets attached to the big sow's nipples. "You like bacon?" her father had said. "That's bacon right there."

It had taken her a long time to decipher Phil's system of morality, and even that understanding was incomplete. If a cashier gave him too much change, he never mentioned the mistake, even if the person seemed very young or very dumb, even if Gina poked him and raised her eyebrows. "How will they learn if I do the math for them?" he reasoned. But at restaurants and stores, he always put spare change into the tins and jars soliciting donations for the Community Kitchen or the Lion's Club or for some kid in Martinsville who needed a kidney. Phil copied computer software but wouldn't tape off CDs, and he offered no convincing reasons as to why one practice was acceptable while the other was not. Was it because software was technology while music was art? Though Gina had spent more than two years with Phil, she still hadn't figured him out.

"We never eat pork chops," said Gina.

"I do," he said. "I eat them at lunch in the cafeteria. I eat them all the time when you're not around."

It was strange to think of, Phil eating pork chops when she wasn't around, one after another, nothing but pork chops. What would he do when she left? "I'm thinking of the people who bought them," she said. "It's not the store that suffers."

The most likely suspects, Phil thought, were the people in front of him in the checkout line, an old couple buying old-people food—saltines and eggs and hard candy, red-and-white peppermints for the grandchildren, yellow-wrapped butterscotches for themselves. The woman wore a tailored coat, the man a suit and tie. They looked like they could get hold of more pork chops if they wanted to. If they really wanted pork chops, Phil decided, they could have them; they could go to a restaurant and order them with mashed potatoes on the side.

"They were old," said Phil, "but they seemed rich or at least comfortable. Anyway"—he held out the unwieldy mass of his keys—"if you feel that strongly, why don't you take them back?" He didn't push the keys in Gina's face or rattle them menacingly; they lay quietly in his opened palm. The relationship might be spiraling downward—it might even be over—but for now they shared a house, a bed, a refrigerator. If he walked on tiptoe and spoke in whispers, she might change her mind. She might decide to stay.

Gina frowned. "You take them back."

"I don't have a problem with them. If it's up to me, I'll keep them."

She stood with her hands on her hips, with the boxes stacked up behind her. "I won't eat them."

"There's tuna," said Phil, flipping through the cookbook. "Turkey, yogurt, eggs. Eat whatever you want."

The pork chops landed on the table with a thud, and Gina left the kitchen. Never the satisfaction of a real fight, she thought. No matter how shrill she got, no matter how nasty, Phil was mild mannered, a compromiser. He was annoying. "Fine, fine, fine," he'd say. And meanwhile, he was making the pork chops; he was doing exactly what he wanted to do.

Of *course* she wouldn't take back the pork chops. They had nothing to do with her. She didn't buy them, she didn't want them, they weren't—were not—her problem. Lying on the couch, she picked up the newspaper, shook out the pages, read.

Phil cut slices of onion and laid the circles flat on a plate. He watched the blade as it sliced through one of the rounds, metal hitting porcelain with a ping. If Gina was in the kitchen now, she'd shake her head and sigh; she'd take the knife from his hand, and he'd have no choice but to stand stupidly by and watch her. She'd have some fast, efficient method—six quick whacks and then sweep the chopped onion into a bowl. Well, she wasn't here now, thought Phil. He could do as he liked.

He imagined the people who'd paid for the pork chops, the old people. Once they got home, they pulled out the heavy black skillet. They melted fat and then reached inside the grocery bag, reached, reached. . . .

Phil wondered if they were the kind of people to turn off the burners and drive back to the store, wave the receipt at the service desk, and demand restitution. Or would they simply resign themselves to the loss and find something else to fry? They'd sit at the table, two old people, eat fried eggs and talk about the pork chops. What could have happened? Had they just plain forgotten to pick them up? No, the receipt said clearly, said without a doubt, that they'd bought them. Oh, well, they thought. Such is life.

Phil wondered what their names might be: Trudy and Oscar or maybe Emily and Warren. No, he decided, they were Millie and Jack, and though they were old, they still enjoyed sex. Sometimes when the weather was mild, they closed all the blinds and went around the house without any clothes on, each at perfect ease with the other's saggy body. Who cared about flab and wrinkles? They loved each other! Sometimes Jack and Millie would stop puttering for an hour or so; they'd lie on the couch or right on the rug and make love. Their children had moved to different states and had good jobs, careers

even. They were gynecologists and economics professors. In the summer the whole family convened at a lake in Michigan for canoeing and
swimming, sun and trout.

What did they need pork chops for? They had afternoon sex and
a lake in Michigan. Phil, meanwhile, had nothing. He had five days
a week of junior high math students. He had Gina bringing home
more boxes every day. "I hope we'll still be friends," she said. "I hope
we'll still do things."

He pushed his fingernail against the clear plastic that was wrapped
around the pork chops. The film stretched, then sagged, then finally
tore. Phil looked at the punctured plastic, the exposed pork chops.
From the living room he heard Gina rattling the newspaper. If she
was reading Ann Landers, she'd be in the kitchen in two minutes.
"Who does Ann Landers think she is?" she'd say, shaking the paper
in Phil's face.

"Don't read it," Phil would advise, and Gina would twist the newspaper into a tube, then slap the table with the mangled pages.

"Everyone reads Ann Landers," she'd say. "How can I not read it?"

Phil would stand quietly and consider his possibilities. If he said,
"You're irrational," she'd say, "I'm leaving." And if he said, "There,
there," she'd leave him anyway. Every option seemed to have the
same outcome: Phil in the kitchen, alone with his pork chops.

Onions, oil, lemon, garlic. Two hours to marinate, then sauté, then
bake. There was plenty of time to venture out for bread. Phil put on
his jacket and went to the garage for his bike. He thought of the first
months after Gina had moved in. On Saturday mornings they used
to bicycle to the bakery and buy a loaf of Amish dill. At home they
boiled a dozen eggs and made a huge vat of egg salad, which they
never came close to finishing. But Phil felt there was an appropriate-
ness to a dozen eggs, the carton full, then empty, the eggs in a single
layer at the bottom of the pan.

Gliding silently on his bike, Phil felt like some kind of nocturnal
animal. He made out details in the darkness—a cat's yellow eyes and

then the brownish orange remains of a pumpkin. Gina had vetoed the idea of Halloween candy when they passed the holiday aisle in the grocery store, and Phil had gone along with her then. But he liked Halloween; he didn't want the holiday to just slip by, just another gray, chilly day. After work on the thirty-first, he stopped at Target and bought an orange plastic pumpkin and a bag of miniature candy bars. He put on the porch light, but as Gina had predicted, no trick-or-treaters came knocking. When the news came on at ten, Gina pointed to the heap of little candy bars. "Now what?"

"We eat them," Phil said, grinning and rubbing his hands together. "We divide them half and half." But Gina didn't want all that candy in the house, and Phil took the plastic pumpkin to school the next day and passed it around in homeroom, to seventh-graders who were already sick from too much candy.

They were going to get married, and now they weren't. They'd been engaged. They'd told people; they'd picked a tentative date, but now she was leaving, and there was nothing Phil could do. He assumed they weren't engaged anymore, but he wasn't sure. Neither of them had issued a statement. When friends asked Phil about the wedding, he said simply, evasively, that they'd hit some snags. He didn't know what Gina said; he wasn't even sure what snags they'd hit. He knew only that she wanted time and space, friends, direction. She'd joined a Masters swim team, and four days a week she went straight from work to the Y. She came home after nine, her hair in wet strings, her skin smelling of chlorine—though she claimed to have taken a shower. "With soap?" asked Phil, and Gina showed him her plastic soap dish, placed his fingers on the wet bar inside. Phil imagined the men she might be swimming with—barrel-chested, hairless men in Speedos—is that what she liked? He pedalled faster just thinking about it. Big-shouldered, slim-waisted men with hair that looked like metal. At first he had tried to fill the swimming hours with tennis, but now it was too cold to coax anyone to play, and he mostly just watched TV or read the paper or planned for the next day's classes.

"Isn't it boring to swim laps?" asked Phil. "Isn't it like walking back and forth in a little room?"

"I think about things," said Gina. "It's not like I leave my brain in the locker room. On the other hand, it's great sometimes to think of nothing at all, to have water all around and quiet."

Phil would imagine floating on his back in a lagoon in the Caribbean, blue sky and water all around. But no matter how appealing Gina's descriptions and his own mental pictures, Phil didn't like to swim. He flailed, he sank, he got water up his nose, and all the next day he sniffled and sneezed.

At the bakery the racks were almost empty. Instead of French bread, Phil had to settle for a homely, lumpy loaf of German rye. He stood for a time in front of the cookie counter. Maybe he should get dessert. What went with pork chops? The cookies were enormous, almost as big as his outstretched hand. If Gina didn't want hers, it would be more than Phil could manage to eat two. He pictured Gina's cookie sitting in its bag on the kitchen counter, getting stale, grease spots showing through the paper. She wouldn't eat the cookie, and neither would Phil, but they wouldn't throw it away either, until it was beyond hard. Or the more likely scenario: she'd move out and leave the cookie, and Phil would be too depressed to ever throw it away. Did Gina even eat cookies now that she was so serious about swimming? Phil didn't know. He didn't know anything about her anymore.

He'd parked his bike in front of the store, and now as he loaded the bread into his backpack, he prayed he wouldn't see anyone he knew. He still loved Bloomington, but lately the town seemed so small and claustrophobic. He'd lived here since his freshman year in college, and he was thirty now. That was twelve years, long enough. He couldn't go anywhere without seeing someone he knew, friends from undergrad days or men he played softball with or fellow teachers at the junior high or even his students. Stop, chat, move along. When Phil and Gina went to their first appointment for couples' counseling, they saw a college friend of Phil's in the hallway of the medical complex. They had to pretend nothing was happening. "Hello!" they'd said. "And what's new with you?"

For months they had talked of being married; they had decided, had gone so far as to look for rings in the mall, but after no more than five minutes of viewing selections, Gina had fled the store. Phil excused himself and wandered the mall looking for her. He saw twenty or thirty women with straight brown hair and jeans shorts, women who could have been Gina, but weren't. There she is, Phil would think, but then she wasn't. He found her finally on a bench outside Penney's, where she was sitting beside a large, yellow potted plant.

"All those names were driving me crazy," said Gina. "Everlasting. Sweetheart. I hated sitting in those purple chairs, and that man with his hair all puffed out, being so helpful and holding out the rings. He was driving me nuts."

Phil wondered how else such a transaction could be managed—he could pick something out and give it to her, the old traditional way, but he wanted Gina to get a ring she liked. Maybe they could look through a catalogue. Once he'd had a girlfriend who left jewelry catalogues lying around his apartment; she'd open the pages to a spread of diamond rings, with circles drawn around the ones she liked. Once she wrote, "Phil will buy me this ring."

But Phil, who was fast losing interest in the woman, wrote, "No, he won't."

"What do we need rings for, anyway?" asked Gina. "If we know we love each other, shouldn't that be enough?"

"Whatever you want," said Phil. "If you don't want one, we won't get one." But gradually Phil realized: it wasn't just the rings.

A few weeks later—six months ago—Gina joined the swim team. She signed up for a Spanish class once a week. On days she didn't swim, she jogged, and sometimes Phil would join her. But more frequently, she left without him, and when he got home from work, she'd be sitting on the floor in the living room, stretching out.

"I would have gone with you," Phil would say, trying to hide his disappointment.

"Oh," Gina would say. "I just wanted to get it over with."

And now she was starting to go out with her new swimming friends. On Saturday mornings they all went out for pancakes, for carbo loading. One night after practice a group of people had drinks and dinner, and Gina didn't come home until eleven. Phil, meanwhile, had waited anxiously, picturing her car spun out of control and smashed against a tree, her spine severed and blood pouring out of her nose. "You're paranoid," she said when he met her on the porch that night.

"I'm not paranoid," said Phil, "but I do worry."

She mentioned names, but she didn't really describe any of her swimming friends, except the coach, Greg, who was spacey and knew Mark Spitz. "Greg says, don't come so much out of the water for butterfly. He says Mark Spitz just did that for pictures, to look cool in pictures.

"Greg said if I had started swimming when I was nine, I could have been a good college swimmer. He says I've got a good feel for the water.

"Should I be disappointed," she asked, "that I didn't swim in college? That I'm twenty-five now and didn't become what I could have become?"

Phil didn't know what amount of regret was appropriate. The only similar situation he could think of was when he was in eighth grade in the all-school spelling bee, and he missed a word on purpose, to avoid the embarrassment of winning. Then in high school he quit the tennis team, but that was because he realized he'd never make varsity. Regret had never seemed like a useful emotion; it just wasted time and made you miserable. If Gina took her boxes and left tomorrow, he'd miss her, but he wouldn't necessarily have regrets. If he got to be eighty years old, though, and never married anyone, if he was living in a trailer and eating beans out of the can, maybe then he'd have regrets. Maybe he'd wish he had spelled that word correctly so many years before: c-o-n-f-e-t-t-i.

Back home Phil parked his bike in the garage. Inside the house he could smell onions and garlic, good, strong smells. Gina was gone— out running, apparently—though he'd asked her many times not to go by herself after dark. He reasoned with her, pleaded with her, but to no avail. "You're crowding me," she said.

If she wanted privacy, Phil thought, if she wanted room to breathe, why couldn't she just move into the second bedroom; why couldn't they just be platonic for a while? She could have her own little space. They could buy groceries separately, maybe just share milk and toilet paper. But what would the parameters be then? If she got a new boyfriend, would she bring him home?

In the early days there hadn't been any problems with closeness, with crowding. Gina and Phil did everything together—jogging, shopping, laundry—everything. But now that Gina was so busy with work and exercise, Phil almost always did the shopping by himself. He changed the sheets on the bed; he cleaned the bathroom, hung up the wet towels. On Sundays while Gina was at church, he made cin- namon rolls with icing. He made them for Gina more than for him- self, and usually she seemed pleased, though sometimes she didn't want them—she'd eaten doughnuts during the community hour af- ter the service.

Gina almost never thanked him. She asked how much the groceries were and gave him half. Sometimes she asked him to buy tampons or deodorant for her, but that was the extent to which she acknowledged how much of the grunt work he'd taken on in recent months. To be honest, he liked the routine, but he would have appreciated a little gratitude nonetheless.

They almost never fought during the time they'd been together. Even now that relations had gotten strained, anger came out in brief spurts—a slammed door, a few sharp words. Most often they spoke calmly, reasonably, with Phil making great efforts to understand

Gina's point of view. But as careful as he tried to be, he still said things he wished he hadn't: "If you're so unhappy," he'd said one night, "maybe you should move out."

"Maybe that's the answer," said Gina. "Maybe I will."

Phil cracked two eggs into a bowl and beat them with a fork. Why didn't she just get on with it, take her boxes and move in with one of her swimming friends, submerge herself completely in that world of wet hair?

Then he thought of himself bent over the toilet, wiping the porcelain with a sponge, and the question reversed itself: Why would she leave?

He filled another bowl with fine bread crumbs, added spices and parmesan cheese, then sifted the grains with his fingers. Why did it keep coming back to what Gina wanted? Why spend all his energy worrying over that question? Why didn't he wonder what he wanted himself?

He wanted to go to a country where parrots would fly past his window, or to a place that still had glaciers. He wanted to walk along the ocean and pick up sand dollars—with Gina if she'd go, and without her if she wouldn't.

He wanted Gina to stop swimming, to stay home, to get old with him.

Sometimes when they sat on the sofa watching TV, Gina would hold out her arm. "Feel my muscles."

He'd press his fingers against her bicep. "Amazing," he'd say.

During the day, Gina would run through the cemetery near their house, but at night the grounds were too isolated, too scary. Most of the nearby roads were busy, and the sidewalks were unreliable, leading into ditches or ending without warning. When she ran at night, Gina circled the block, around and around, past the same houses until she'd logged four miles. When she moved, she'd live in town, closer to the center of things, and she could run on the high school track. It would be the same thing, running around in circles, but she'd feel less silly somehow.

She'd found a place; she'd signed the lease. He must have guessed about the boxes. It was so strange to think about: they were going to get married—they had interviewed caterers and discussed rice pilaf—and now she was moving out. She hoped they would stay friends, maybe even date, spend Saturday nights watching TV, hanging out.

The air was chilly but comfortable, and her pace was steady, a bit slower than usual. She felt good, though; she felt strong. She was ready to move on. She had her futon, her answering machine, her dishes, her papasan chair. She'd be paying more for rent than she paid now, but financially she'd be okay. She worked as a secretary at a law firm, and though the job itself was rather grim, the pay was reasonable; the benefits were good.

Of course, Phil was the one who first suggested that she move. And once the idea was out on the table, he certainly hadn't made efforts to convince her to stay. He hadn't done anything except turn into a neat freak overnight, bleaching out the kitchen sink every day and changing the sheets two times a week. She couldn't even use a glass in the kitchen without him washing it as soon as she was finished. And the pork chops—weren't they just another way to annoy her, another way for Phil to prove that he was in the driver's seat?

And yet, how could any of this be Phil's doing? After all, he was the one who wanted them to try counseling. She was the one who couldn't find the time after the first two sessions, after the therapist said, "Some couples decide that they don't have enough common ground for a lasting relationship."

No matter how Gina sliced up the situation, no matter how she arranged the facts, she was the one who wanted to leave. She was the one who panicked in the jewelry store. All that talk of pear cuts and facets, settings and carats and prongs, all the words that conveyed the same terrifying message: forever forever forever.

"We want good value," Phil had said, and that's when her insides seized up, when she ran away, had to run.

She thought of what the swim coach had said—she could have been a college swimmer. She was trying to decide whether she had regret. She wished she'd had the excitement, the camaraderie. But she wondered, can you regret something you never really had a chance at? It wasn't as if she'd been a swimmer and then gave it up because she was lazy or started smoking pot every day. It wasn't as if someone had given her a plane ticket to France, and she'd been afraid to use it, afraid that her French wasn't good enough. Would she regret not marrying Phil? She didn't think so, but it was so hard to know for sure. Maybe they'd still get married. Maybe this was just what they needed, time to think and room to breathe.

Gina turned off Park onto Nancy Lane. Though it was just the first week in November, the house on the corner was blazing with Christmas lights. There was a green plastic sleigh in the yard with an illuminated Santa perched on the seat. The edges of both sleigh and Santa were blurry, as if obscured by a snowstorm, though the night was clear, not even foggy.

She couldn't explain what had happened to the relationship. It wasn't until the moment she said she'd marry Phil that she realized she didn't want to. Now she thought back to the day they'd met, a cold afternoon in February at the counter of Mr. Copy, where she'd gone to get résumés printed, and Phil was copying his tax return.

Over coffee she told him how she'd come to Bloomington to get a master's in English, how she'd dropped out of the program after one miserable semester. And Phil just listened; he let her talk. Unlike the rest of the world, he didn't bombard her with suggestions about careers she should consider: Have you thought of going to library school? What about nursing? That night they went to a movie, and on the weekend they went ice skating. Before a month had gone by, they moved in together, or, rather, Gina moved her things into Phil's house.

It was fun back then: Phil planned picnics to the quarries and long bike rides in the country; he made her a piñata; he bought her a cactus. One weekend they drove up to Chicago on a whim, ate Indian food and visited the aquarium. They'd walked down busy streets in the brisk air, and Gina remembered throwing her hat up, like Mary Tyler Moore, giddy and happy, and then catching it again.

He told her he'd become a teacher in part for the summers off, so he could travel, and Gina had admired his foresight, his adventurousness. He liked to go to travel agencies and bring home booklets about cruises and safaris and wine tours of France, but Gina realized soon enough that he never advanced beyond reading. He never actually went anywhere, except occasionally to Evansville to visit his parents. Once or twice a year he went to the post office and got forms for a passport, but he never finished filling them out.

Of course, thought Gina, these were petty complaints, excuses that would sound foolish if she spoke them aloud. "I'm leaving you because you don't have a passport." "I'm leaving you because you change the sheets too often." She couldn't help it, though. She didn't want her life to be so ordered and so dull: groceries on Thursday, laundry on Friday, egg salad on Saturday.

She thought of the night a few months ago when she'd come home from swimming, still buzzing from the adrenaline of the final sprint, still replaying her flip turn, her push off the wall, her burst of speed. She found Phil slumped in an armchair that had been pulled close to the TV. His legs were stuck out straight in front of him; his hands were folded on his chest. He was watching a car race, absolutely motionless, a television zombie.

"Don't you have anything better to do?" asked Gina.

"I guess not," he said, and he still didn't move.

Back on the porch Gina cleaned the mud off her shoes on the dirty doormat. Phil was back, and the house smelled wonderful. He didn't say anything when she came in. Gina sat on the floor in the living room and stretched. It had been cool outside, so she wasn't too sweaty. She could get by without a shower.

This is how it would be when she lived alone. No one would call out to her from the kitchen when she came back from running. There wouldn't be this smell of cooking, but there would be quiet and calm. There would be room for her to stretch out; she could take half an hour if she wanted to. She'd go swimming and then eat pancakes. She'd study Spanish. She'd go to work. Every once in a while she'd call Phil and see how he was doing. That would be her life, and she would be happy. She stood and pressed her hands against the wall, stretching her calves, then wandered into the kitchen, where Phil was snapping green beans. She inhaled deeply, with her eyes closed. "Yum," she said.

"I can set you a plate," said Phil.

"Look at this bread." Gina pulled off a chunk, smelled it, then ate it.

Phil decided he wouldn't push; he wouldn't ask her again, but he'd set her place at the table. He'd say "Dinner" like it was nothing, like he was saying "Phone's for you" or "You got a letter." And she would eat. And she would stay. He should have gotten ice cream—mint chocolate chip or coffee—but he hadn't thought of it until right now. He hadn't realized how important it might be.

"It smells really really good in here," said Gina.

"Just a few more minutes." Phil dropped the beans into the pan and put on the lid.

At the last minute he put candles on the table, turned off the overhead light in the dining room and switched on a smaller lamp. When she sat at the table, Phil passed her the platter of pork chops. He was nice enough not to tease her.

"These are great," said Gina, chewing. "I don't even like pork chops."

Phil described the recipe he'd followed: the marinade and the breading, then sauté and bake. "The green beans are just steamed, and of course, I bought the bread."

"Delicious."

If she was going to make her announcement, he didn't have to make it easy for her. If he made it hard enough for her to say she was leaving, maybe she'd decide to stay. Phil could dream up some elaborate plot, like putting an engagement ring at the bottom of a bowl of chocolate pudding, and they could try again—they could fall in love again.

"You know," said Phil, "all the famous swimmers eat pork chops—Diana Nyad ate pork chops."

"Who's Diana Nyad?"

"You call yourself a swimmer? Didn't you watch that movie in school? She swam to Cuba. She ate a lot of food before she went. The object, I think, is to make yourself look like a dolphin so that you blend in with the rest of the ocean."

Gina laughed. She ripped off another chunk of bread, and watching her chew, Phil could see the future. After they ate they'd settle in on the couch. They'd kiss to try to taste the flavors on each other's lips—garlic, lemon, onion, oil—and from kissing they'd drift seamlessly into sex.

"Did she make it to Cuba?" asked Gina.

"I don't think so. I think she ran into sharks."

"You know," said Gina, "I've been thinking. So what if I wasn't a college swimmer? I'm not a ballerina either. Or a chemist."

"That's true," said Phil. "I wouldn't worry about it."

"It's stupid, I guess, to spend so much time swimming." She stuck her finger to the plate to pick up bread crumbs that had fallen off. "What's it for? I'll still be twenty-five. I can't change that. I can't go back to college."

"It's not stupid if you like it."

"I do like it."

"Then why is it stupid?"

Gina held up her plate and looked sheepish. "Can I have another pork chop?"

After they ate they turned on the TV and sat on the sofa, and one thing followed another, just as Phil had imagined. They kissed first, savoring the taste of meat and garlic, and then they made love with the sounds of CNN in the background: Bosnia, Haiti, unemployment, housing starts. Phil was polite; he was careful. He ran his hand over Gina's back, but he waited for her to unhook her bra herself. He waited for her to move her hand to his pants. But once Phil was inside her, he felt fierce, not gentle. He pushed into her hard, pushed as far as he could go. Maybe he was trying to hurt her, but she wrapped her legs around him and moved with him. When Phil looked down at Gina, her eyes were closed, and she was smiling, and he loved her. He loved her.

*A*fterward, Gina stood in the shower humming "Sleigh Ride" as hot water ran over her body. She soaped herself once and rinsed off, then soaped herself again just so she could stay longer in the warmth of the water. She felt comfortable, happy, almost free.

Often in the past she'd moved from boyfriend to boyfriend, without leaving any gaps. But now there was no one on the horizon, no cowboy on a white horse. She saw a clear space out in front of her where she could be by herself. She could think about the things that needed to be thought about. She could quit her job and go to Spain, eat paella and sleep in monasteries. She could go to Aspen and work in a ski lodge.

As for Phil, it was just—was it wrong to feel this way?—she didn't need him anymore.

In the living room, Phil sat alone on the sofa. He felt as if his insides had been scraped out, even though she'd kissed him on the nose just before she stood up. He thought of how he'd been afraid that Gina would get shoulders like the East German women swimmers. But

Gina, while she certainly got stronger, also got sleeker, sexier. It was steroids that made the East Germans look so misshapen. Swimming alone didn't have such an effect. Swimming made her beautiful.

He knew this was just the moment she was waiting for. Some moment she could call an ending, a special evening to remind her why she'd loved him in the first place. She'd be gone next week, or she'd be gone in the morning. And as time passed she'd forget how they used to ride their bikes to the bakery and to the park; she'd forget her suggestion that they still be friends. She'd forget the head-spinning taste of the pork chops. She'd tell people that Phil had stolen them; she'd say he forced her to eat them, that she hated pork chops.

When Phil heard the bedroom door close, he went into the bathroom. Opening the door he released a cloud of steam. The floral fragrance was from Gina's shampoo, but he couldn't help thinking he was breathing in her essence. She'd hung her wet washcloth on the edge of the tub to dry, and he picked it up. He laid the cloth on his face and breathed in the smell of her soap, her skin. He was smelling soap and crying, sitting on the side of the tub in the steamy intimacy of the bathroom, his body heaving with the force of his sobs. There was nothing to be done. She was going. She was gone.

In bed Gina was asleep already, warm and washed and dreaming. She was moving steadily through the water, over waves and under waves, swimming out to sea.

After scanning the bar codes and stacking the books, Ann May said what she always said: "These are due back in three weeks."

But the short man in the plaid cap didn't nod and take his books. Instead, he stood in front of the checkout desk with his hands jammed in his jacket pockets. He looked at Ann May, and she felt her face go red. She felt the itch of her sweater against her neck.

The massive oak desk formed a barrier as thick as the walls of a fortress, and as primitive. Perched on her high stool, Ann May was tall enough to see the cloth-covered button on top of the man's cap, the fine purple veins that threaded through his ears; she was taller than the man, and yet she didn't feel imposing.

She pushed his books across the shiny expanse of wood, until the spines were parallel with the edge of the desk. His library card, a slim rectangle of white plastic, crowned the pile—if he was waiting for his card, there it was.

If he had fines to pay, she would have told him. If he wanted dimes for the copy machine, or quarters for the bus, she couldn't help.

Go on, now, she wanted to say. Go.

The library was hot and smelled like old footballs. Zigzags of sweat ran from Ann May's armpits down her sides, stopping when they soaked in at the waistband of her pants. Her long hair was loose down her back and heavy as an army blanket—she wished she'd pulled it into a ponytail, or somehow smoothed it into submission. She wished she knew how she looked. When Julie, the other desk clerk, was around, she often served as a human mirror, tabulating and announcing Ann May's flaws. She liked to hold up her fingers and tick off Ann May's weak spots: "You need lipstick and mascara and a *stylish* haircut. Bangs or wisps or something. And moisturizer! You're flaking!"

Of course, now that Ann May actually needed Julie's help, Julie was nowhere to be seen. Off flirting, thought Ann May. Off combing her hair.

Not that Julie needed much upkeep on her appearance: she always looked great, with rose shadows on her eyelids, and straight, brown hair that was purposely asymmetrical. It's much easier to be pretty when you're sixteen, Ann May wanted to say. You wait and see.

The man hadn't moved—maybe hadn't breathed. He blinked and blinked again. Trying for a brisk, professional tone, Ann May produced a croak, a whisper. "Thank you."

The man gave a faint smile then ran his tongue over his front teeth, the way people did in toothpaste commercials. Ann May wondered if he'd recently been to the dentist and was still getting used to the slick, porcelain feel of clean teeth. He looked as if he was going to say something—his lips fell apart slightly. Ann May waited, but he didn't speak; he only stared, and she cringed to think that people might be watching. Turning toward the computer, she pretended to type in data: "library desk, Tuesday, eieidd, ightishe, eithete." Tap, tap, tap. If he glanced at the screen, he would see that the typing was nonsense, but she took the risk—she had to do something. She never should have accepted the promotion to desk clerk. The tiny raise in pay wasn't worth the aggravation, the cranky and crazy and persistent people. She wished she was still working as a page in the library basement, shelving and retrieving books; for years she'd been perfectly happy as an anonymous peon. As a page she could spend the entire day inside herself, speaking to no one and carrying books.

The library was noisy, as it almost always was. Shuffles and clicks of the copy machine, the murmur of high school students huddled over chemistry problems and *Cliffs Notes*. A high-pitched squeal prickled Ann May's skin: the squeak of the paperback rack as a patron turned it to view the selections—dozens of tattered romances with bosomy heroines on the covers. Sometimes when Ann May was alone in the back room, loading or unloading the book carts, she would flip quickly through one of these books, searching for sexy scenes, scanning the pages for key words: rapture, desire, fire, rod, rapier, release.

The truth was, she'd never even kissed a man, aside from the unavoidable, embarrassing pecks exchanged with relatives at the holidays. Thirty-three, unmarried, a virgin—still, she hadn't abandoned all hope. At home in her bed, she sometimes slid her hand under the covers and touched her body in its soft places, dreaming of lean men who sang James Taylor songs to her. She read the personal ads in the newspaper, imagining candles and moonlight and scuba for two. She noticed that most of the ads discouraged replies from overweight women. But Ann May was slim; she had that going for her.

She tapped the keys. Though she tried to focus on the movement of her fingers and the gibberish on the screen, she knew he was still there, still standing, still staring. Without looking, she could see his sturdy legs, his solid torso. His jacket was zipped up; his eyebrows were thick and dark. The skin under his chin sagged slightly.

The man coughed, and Ann May lifted her head. His cheeks were pink, and his ears stuck out prominently. "What's your name?" he asked, and Ann May told him.

When the library closed that night, Ann May walked home down Main, past shadows and parked cars, past hunched figures inside the plastic bubble of the bus stop. Across the street, a lone fireman sat on a chair in the driveway outside the firehouse. He lifted his hand in a silent wave, and Ann May waved back. At night the firefighters always waved or nodded, and Ann May thought the greetings to be vaguely religious; the waves were blessings that said, "Be safe and remember, don't play with fire."

As a child Ann May had been terrified of the dark. She was afraid of people lurking in the bushes, afraid people would pull her into their big, rusty cars. On summer nights she'd stayed inside after dinner when her siblings went out for a final round of play. Even now, so many years later, she felt uncomfortable walking the silent streets. Of course, the possibility of crime seemed greater these days—though she hadn't heard of much happening in this neighborhood. In any event, she would have welcomed a ride home, but in the eighteen years she'd worked at the library, her parents had seldom offered. Even on the coldest nights, even when it snowed, she walked alone down Main Street. Often she thought of running home—she wanted to run. Julie ran; sometimes she even ran from her high school to the library, showing up flushed and healthy looking, in colorful stretch tights and sweaty T-shirts, and then disappearing into the restroom. Three or four minutes later Julie was cleaned and groomed and ready to work. Ann May was not nearly that free spirited; she felt self-conscious, even in the dark. She was a foot in a shoe, tuna in a can, confined, restricted—the best she could do was walk quickly, heel-toe, heel-toe, feeling the big muscles in her buttocks burn, feeling ropes wrap around her chest, tighter and tighter.

His name was Jerry, and that was all she knew, besides his clothes, his features, his voice, his books, the scant information she'd gathered in her glances. "I've seen you working here," he'd said, and she hadn't known what to respond. He was right—the front desk at the library was where she worked. When he tried to give her his business card, she pushed it back to him, sliding it along the glossy wood and shaking her head. But as he lifted his books—finally—from the counter and turned to go, Ann May had managed a whisper: "I don't work on Thursdays." She didn't know why she'd said that.

After he left, Julie appeared from wherever she'd been, poking and nudging and speaking in a singsong, a teasing, childish, playground voice. "He likes you, Ann May. I think he likes you."

With a quick, hard elbow jab, Ann May pushed her away. Then turning to her computer, she moved the bright green dot of the cursor backward, across the screen and up, erasing what she'd written and holding in a smile.

At home Ann May crept up to her room, tiptoeing past the closed door of her parents' bedroom. Once her own door was shut, she eased herself onto the floor, sitting, then lying with her back against the worn celery carpet. Knees bent, feet flat. She got herself into position before she had time to wonder what she was doing, before she had time to stop herself. With her hands behind her head, she tried to pull herself up into a sit-up, but she couldn't seem to keep her feet connected with the floor. In junior high gym class, she remembered, they'd worked with partners, one girl holding another girl's feet down. But alone in her bedroom, Ann May was stymied, she was stuck; she opened her mouth and closed it. She had hated junior high, and gym class had been especially excruciating. In the locker room, she'd tried to dress as quickly as possible, but there was always a moment when she was naked and vulnerable. Once she'd had her period, and her sanitary napkin, fastened to its prehistoric security belt, had leaked and soaked her underwear; Ann May had been mortified, but she'd had no choice except to change into her gym suit, to run around for an hour with blood darkening her navy blue shorts, trying to whack a chalkboard eraser with a hockey stick. She remembered girls pointing, laughing, whispering.

Lying on the floor in her bedroom, she remembered another time in junior high—eighth grade. She'd been outside with a group of girls in the neighborhood, girls who had accepted her presence since kindergarten without any major rebuffs, when suddenly they turned on her. It started when Jessica Embry threw a stone—a piece of driveway gravel—at her, casually, as if by accident. "Oh, sorry," she said. Briget followed suit, tossed a stone. Then Peggy. Even Lee Ann threw a stone. They started a chant: "Ann May doesn't shave her legs, Ann May doesn't shave her legs." Rocks smacked her shins, bounced down and hit her feet. Then a barrage of taunts—"Ann May stinks, Ann May stinks, Ann May doesn't wipe her butt." On and on, and rocks bouncing all around her and sometimes hitting her—sometimes hurting. They stood in a circle surrounding her, voices growing louder and more shrill, while she cried and covered her face until finally Mrs. Lavalette, a neighbor lady, came out of her house and shouted at them. "You're terrible," she told them. "Do you want me to throw rocks at you? Go home. Get out of here." When the other girls had slunk away, Mrs. Lavalette asked Ann May if she was okay. Ann May nodded and wiped her nose. "You go home, too," said Mrs. Lavalette. "Go on home."

Her parents had attended to her cuts and scrapes but sidestepped the real source of Ann May's misery. "Feel better?" her mother asked when the wounds were cleaned and bandaged, and Ann May nodded yes.

Later that year Ann May's English class read "The Lottery." In her bedroom, reading the story, Ann May had cried so hard her eyelids puffed up, threatening to swell shut. The next day, the day the class was supposed to discuss the story, Ann May refused to go to school. She stayed home eating saltines and tomato soup, listening to her brothers' Beatles records, and hugging her arms around her knees.

She tried another sit-up, failed again. This must be it, she thought—middle age. From now on her body would just get more and more decrepit. She lay with the back of her head resting in her hands and prepared to give in to the inevitable. Then, catching sight of the bed, Ann May got the idea to hook her feet under the frame; her bed became her partner, providing leverage and stability. After ten sit-ups she relaxed and kneaded the muscles of her abdomen, feeling pleased with herself and relieved, as well, that she hadn't woken anyone—she hoped she hadn't woken anyone.

She thought of how she'd always gone through life—quiet and fearing reprimands. When Ann May's brothers passed through adolescence, they'd screeched the tires of their cars, thrown the sticks from their drum sets against the wall, peed off the second-floor roof into the backyard. Her younger sister, Monica, had gotten pregnant when she was a senior in high school. Meanwhile, Ann May had practically given herself ulcers trying to be good, or at least anonymous. And now she was here, thirty-three, afraid to do a sit-up, afraid someone might find out. Lying on the floor in her bedroom, Ann May began to think she could get away with more than she'd ever thought possible. She might get away with anything she tried.

He walked in the door, but he didn't say hello. Ann May watched him head toward the back of the library, then turn left into the stacks—Biographies, Finance, Sports. He walked as if he knew what he wanted, as if he knew the shelves by heart.

Ann May had to admit, working at the front desk did have some advantages. It was easier to people-watch, easier to eavesdrop. And once she'd developed formulas for handling the routine transactions, she alleviated some of her most paralyzing fear. Sometimes she could tell that other people were as frightened as she was. These people brought out the extrovert in her; she would smile and say, "Have a nice day!" Sometimes the person checking out a book was someone she knew—someone from her grade school or high school, neighbors or fellow parishioners from St. Jude, friends of her parents or her siblings. She even recognized a few people from her days at community college, where she'd taken classes for a semester.

Sometimes Ann May would ask these people she vaguely knew if they had liked the books they'd just returned. Each sentence was an effort, and often she felt foolish, always she felt awkward, but she measured her progress against her past, and she knew—even if others did not—that there had been a time when she would not have been able to say anything.

Ann May sat with her hands on her lap. Julie was hunched over one of the free alternative newspapers she'd picked up off the floor at the front door of the library, papers Ann May almost never read. "You know the Weird News section?" asked Julie.

Ann May nodded.

"Here's a story about a guy who got arrested in Albuquerque for scalping women. What he'd do was, he'd meet a woman at the park or somewhere, then he'd scalp her and put the hair in a plastic bag in his bread box and keep it."

"Did the women die?"

"It doesn't say," said Julie.

Ann May scanned the library, taking note of the patrons. Once she thought she spotted Jerry passing between two rows of books, but she couldn't be sure it was him. She wondered how reliable the news could be in a free newspaper. It seemed like real news should cost something.

"Here's one about a guy in England who strangled his mother because she wouldn't let him watch a soccer match on TV."

"That's weird," Ann May murmured, only half listening now as she watched Jerry approach, as she followed the pink-and-white pinstripes weaving through the tables.

Julie looked up; a sly smile crossed her face, and she gave Ann May's hand a hard pinch. "Go for it."

"I'm not helping him," said Ann May. "It's your turn." But Julie had turned toward the wall, to a file box filled with orange index cards; she refused to look up.

And then he was standing in front of her—stripes, jacket, cap, teeth. Jerry. He put a book on the counter, and Ann May ran it through the scanner. Avoiding eye contact she looked down, allowing her hair to cover her face. When she straightened she dragged the mass of hair back over her shoulder. Her face was bare, unprotected. Was her nose greasy? Was she flaking?

"You're a fast reader," she whispered, her face flaming at the effort of speaking the sentence. She knew Julie was listening—probably watching, too.

"Too much time on my hands." He winked and was gone.

Ann May felt a hand on her shoulder, hot breath in her ear—Julie whispering—"He's in love. He's in L-O-V-E."

Mornings, Ann May woke early—five o'clock or sometimes six. She lay in bed studying the ceiling, her limbs inert and heavy and sinking deep into the mattress. The ugly brown watermark above had been painted over twelve or fifteen times, but it was showing through again. She was reluctant to mention the discoloration to her father. Though she chipped in a hundred and seventy-five dollars each month for rent, though she tried to live quietly and eat lightly, she was certain her parents had grown tired of her being around. Ever since she finished high school, she'd half expected them to present her with an eviction notice, a gentle nudge, but however many years later, here she was, a household fixture—as permanent as the china cabinet, as familiar as the old rag rug in the hall. If they asked her to leave, she'd understand. She'd look for an apartment; go to garage sales and Goodwill and buy the things she'd need: dish drainer, pot holders, spoons.

As she lay in bed, Ann May thought of running. In her mind she went through the necessary procedures—pull off the blankets, put on loose pants, tie back her hair. Downstairs, she'd open the door, hold the handle so that it clicked quietly back into place. Then she was down the steps, taking in air that was misty—chilled, but not too cold—breathing gracefully, effortlessly through her nose, like a horse, and her feet barely touched the ground as she skimmed lightly over grass and pavement. She was running, she was running!

But ugly pictures intruded—her brothers yelling out of car windows at slow joggers: "I could walk faster than that!" Her brothers weren't in the city anymore, they weren't in high school anymore, but they weren't the only mean, bored people in the world. Did she really want to submit herself to that? Was the pleasure of running worth the probable humiliation?

And so she stayed in bed until she heard her parents opening doors and flushing toilets.

While her mother measured quick oats, Ann May made coffee. She loved the harsh sound of the grinder as it pulverized the beans, the quick transformation of hard, shiny pellets into dust.

Her father lowered the newspaper. "Read any good books?" he asked. It was the same greeting he'd used since she began working at the library, and the joke's funniness had faded long ago.

"Nope," said Ann May. "Not in a while." The truth was that she read books all the time, and liked most of them.

Her mother stirred the cereal and talked about Ann May's sister in San Diego, about her brothers and their wives. Listening, nodding, setting out the bowls, Ann May thought of an odd encounter she'd had with her mother a few years before.

She'd been in the basement loading the washer when her mother came down the stairs. Walking past Ann May to the dryer, she pulled out the lint screen and solemnly scraped off the blue-gray layer that had accumulated. "If you're a lesbian," she said in a loud voice, "I'll still love you. I want you to know that." Then she set the lint wad delicately on the dryer and went back upstairs without looking at Ann May, without giving Ann May a chance to say she wasn't, that she wouldn't—

Now Ann May unwound the twist tie from the bread bag and mentioned the article Julie had read aloud the night before, about the man who'd been arrested for scalping his dates. "He met them in Albuquerque," she said. "In parks."

"If you want to run," said Julie, "just do it." Her hands flew up as if to indicate that it was just that easy. "Go tomorrow morning and then at work you can tell me if you liked it."

"I'm out of shape," Ann May protested. "I'd be wheezing. I'd fall down."

Julie clamped her hand over Ann May's mouth. "I don't want to hear it. Just go."

So the next morning, when Ann May's alarm sounded, she stood up, she dressed, she went outside—she ran. It was harder than she thought it would be, but also exhilarating. Alternating running and walking, she went twice around Loose Park, and no one screamed at her. In fact, the only people she saw were other walkers and joggers, and they'd all smiled and said good morning.

When Julie asked, Ann May said she'd gotten up early and taken a walk. "That's okay," said Julie. "That's a start."

Ann May was on her dinner break, walking south on Main, when a car scraped the curb, pulling up next to her. The passenger door flew open, and she jumped back to avoid getting hit. When she looked at the person leaning half over the seat, waving at her, she saw it was Jerry. His eyebrows lifted, his lips formed the word, "Supper?" and before she could think, she filled her lungs with air, climbed into the car, and closed the door. "Go for it," Julie had said. "Go for it."

Jerry looked at Ann May, then turned forward and smiled. "Hey, hey!" he said. "What do you know?"

Ann May's throat was sucked out and dry. She was in his car and he was pulling away from the curb and he was driving and she was in his car. She was mute as an eggplant, and she was in his car.

"Just because you're a virgin doesn't mean you have to stay one," Julie had said, and though Ann May thought about sex, read about sex, dreamed about sex, she wasn't ready; she wasn't ready to be in Jerry's car. She hardly even knew him. She hadn't shaved her legs since September. And wouldn't she need new underwear?

She clutched the door handle. He could do anything to her, and no one would know. Unless he scalped her, her parents would have no idea of what had happened to her—even then they'd be confused. Except for Albuquerque, they'd have no clues.

Jerry slapped the steering wheel with both hands. "Okay!" he said. "This is lucky. This is great!"

Two blocks past the library, Jerry turned into the parking lot at Winstead's. He pulled forward until the tires bumped the concrete parking barrier. "Crash landing," he said, laughing awkwardly, and Ann May began to relax. "Supper," he'd said. Supper she could handle.

He rolled down his window but didn't get out of the car, and Ann May realized that they weren't going inside, that they were going to eat in the parking lot. Why not go inside, she wondered, but then she was relieved—out here no one would see her. Jerry affixed the microphone to his window and handed Ann May a menu.

She drove a bitten-down fingernail into the flesh of her thumb and planned what she would say. It wouldn't be fair to make him do all the talking. His job, where did he work? Should she ask if he was divorced? It was possible that he was married. What were the appropriate questions? Julie's frequent references to sex hadn't included any tips on how to conduct a conversation with a man.

Ann May stared out behind Winstead's where the tennis courts used to be. They were ripped up now, along with half the city, part of a dubious improvement project that involved waterways and gondolas. When Ann May was eleven she had taken four sweaty weeks of tennis lessons at these courts. It was strange to think about: Julie wasn't even born then, but in many ways she seemed older than Ann May. Use moisturizer! Go for it!

"Once I came here," said Jerry, "and I ordered the skyscraper soda. That's for four people it says on the menu, but I ordered it myself and I finished it.

"This was with a girl I knew then—to impress her, you know, and by the time I got to the bottom of the glass, she was pretty damned impressed. Excuse my French."

He held on to the steering wheel while he talked and stared straight out ahead of him. He had thick, dark hair growing on his fingers and on the backs of his hands, furry hands that made Ann May think of bear paws. "You're a quiet person," said Jerry. "I like that." Ann May didn't know how to respond to his comment, except to keep quiet.

He touched her lightly on the knuckle, brushing her skin with the tip of his index finger. "You're pretty."

Ann May didn't say anything. She knew she wasn't pretty; she knew her face was drab and pale. Her hair was thick and brown. It was long but not sleek and lovely the way some women's hair was. Her hair was just there.

"Do you ever wear green?" Jerry put his hand out and touched her hair. "You'd look great in green."

Ann May shook her head. "Not usually." She felt as if she'd stepped outside herself. She was watching from a distance as Jerry's hand moved through her hair, his heavy, hairy hand was stroking her. He was painting a picture of her, but when she looked at the canvas, it wasn't her. His composition was shadowy, pretty, vague; it wasn't her. He looked at her for a long while, his eyes steady and fixed on her face, while Ann May glanced here and there, taking note of the dashboard, the parking stickers, avoiding his gaze.

"Do you have any hobbies?" she asked.

Back at work, she was five minutes late, but no one noticed except Julie. Ann May took her place at the desk, her heart still pounding, her breathing audible—at least to her. She checked out a stack of books, she answered a question on the telephone, she settled into her work, into dreams, into remembering how he looked, how his arms were covered with hair, how his finger was rough when he touched her hand—but warm.

At Ann May's request Jerry had dropped her off opposite the library, at the corner. As she was crossing, the light turned yellow, and she'd had to scurry across. For a few steps she was running. She loved the danger and excitement of it—the fleeting feeling of being alive.

They began meeting regularly for dinner. Just after six Ann May would set off walking, and Jerry would pull alongside the curb and open the door. She never looked at him until she was in the car with her seat belt fastened. Only then, when she was committed to being there, the car rolling forward, would she turn her head and say hello.

She took to leaving a note in the pocket of her sweater, which she left hanging on a hook in the cloakroom at the library: "Ann May is having dinner with Jerry Glenn. He drives a brown Honda, license plate number 53B 487K."

She wrote the date—10-13, 10-14, 10-15, crossing out each day to make room for the next so that the notes began to look like scoresheets. Did ten dates mean they were a couple? How many dates before they were in love?

For oral sex you want a nonlubricated condom," said Julie, "but otherwise, get the lubricated kind—you'll be glad you did."

"How do you know all this?" asked Ann May.

Julie rolled her eyes. "I'm sexually active. I've been on the pill since I was thirteen."

Ann May nodded calmly, but her head felt as if it were about to explode. Thirteen! When Ann May was thirteen, she was shuffling through the halls of her high school in a plaid uniform skirt that went past her knees. She was turning bright red when she ordered chicken breast at a restaurant.

"Don't have a heart attack," said Julie. "I was practically the last virgin in my school—except for the real freaks." She stopped, laughed, backtracked. "Not that you're a freak or anything. You're just shy. You're a victim of circumstance." She patted Ann May's arm, and Ann May stiffened.

"You know, there's this girl in my school, and she wears a little gold cross on a necklace—her father gave it to her, and it means she's going to stay a virgin until she gets married. She says she's a 'voluntary virgin.' Besides that, though, she's perfectly normal, she's just this girl. She's a JV cheerleader and plays volleyball and everything. People say, 'What if you never get married?' and she just laughs. 'Don't worry about it,' she says."

A woman with two children and a brown grocery bag full of books began sliding volume after volume through the book drop. Ann May and Julie filled their arms and walked toward the back room, where the sorting carts were stored.

"What's it like?" Ann May whispered. Her face was burning, and she felt the hard corners of books pressing into her arms.

"It's no big deal. Kind of slippery. It's good if you like the guy."

One night at dinner Jerry presented her with a flat, white box from Dillard's. They were sitting in the car at Winstead's, waiting for their food to arrive.

"Open it," he said excitedly. "Open it!" He lifted one end of the lid while Ann May lifted the other. Inside she found a kelly green silk blouse with puffy peasant sleeves.

"Trust me," said Jerry. "Green is your color." He held the fabric to her face and smiled. "It's you!"

He kissed her then for the first time. She saw his nose coming closer, closer, until his pores seemed magnified, until her eyes were focused on a single pore, with its tiny center of blackness. She held the blouse in her hands. His lips felt damp and colder than she'd expected, and she wanted to jerk her head away at the contact. But she held herself steady and pushed her lips to meet his.

"The more I know you, the more I like you," said Jerry.

The fabric was soft; its color was vibrant. She settled the blouse back into its box, then lifted it out again.

"I have to tell you something," said Jerry, and he waited until she'd packed the present away. "You should know this," he said, and then he looked at her. He spoke solemnly and held the steering wheel with both hands. "I only have one ball—you know, one testicle."

He seemed to be waiting for a response.

"That's okay," she said.

"I'm not sterile or anything. I just thought you might want to know."

"It's okay with me," said Ann May, but she wondered, would it make a difference? It must matter, she thought, or he wouldn't have mentioned it.

"I hope you like the shirt," said Jerry.

"It's great," she said, and he put his arms around her and pulled her close. She could hear the thump of his heart in his chest, the slight whistle of his breathing. She supposed she'd have to tell him sometime; she might as well tell him now.

Moving her mouth close to his ear, Ann May whispered her secret: "I'm a virgin."

Jerry pushed back a little and looked at her. He put his hand on her chin so that she had to look at him, too. "I thought you probably were," he said.

At the library, Julie pulled the shirt out of its box. "Put it on. God, it's gorgeous."

The library had four public restrooms, which were labeled Boys,

Girls, Women, Men. Ann May went into the women's room. In her early teens, she'd agonized over the choices. She didn't know where the cutoff was; she'd gotten her period early, at age eleven, too young to fathom the idea of being a woman. But if not then, when? When a boy kissed her, when she shaved her legs, when she got a purse, when she had sex? Often Ann May avoided the problem by waiting until she got home to use the restroom. But when she was fifteen, she started working at the library, and she had to make a decision.

In the narrow stall, Ann May hung the blouse on the purse hook while she removed her own shirt. It's you, he'd said, but he was wrong. She was black turtleneck sweaters. She was white blouses with Peter Pan collars, white blouses with yellow stains under the arms.

She examined herself in the mirror, straightened the collar, but the flimsy material had no substance and the collar drooped. The sleeves were huge and puffy.

She'd always associated presents with embarrassment. When she was a child, her parents had given her clothes at Christmas and birthdays. A crocheted poncho, an orange plaid two-piece swimsuit—nothing had been quite right, but she'd had to go upstairs and try them on anyway, troop down and model, smile and thank her parents: "It's great. I love it."

She thought of the man a few years ago who for a month had left her little presents—peppermints, erasers, coupons for lessons at Arthur Murray. She had just started working at the front desk then, and she remembered how idiotic she'd felt when her fellow desk worker—not Julie then—would watch the man sidle up and deposit his offering. Ann May had finally resorted to hiding in the back room when she saw the man approaching, and eventually he stopped bothering her, though she still saw him in the library sometimes.

Ann May felt ridiculous when she came out of the restroom; she felt conspicuous, as if a spotlight were following her as she made her way. At the desk Julie stroked her sleeve, petting Ann May's arm as if it were a poodle.

"Okay," said Ann May and moved her arm.

"Silk's expensive," said Julie. "He must really like you."

Sometimes they would skip Winstead's and drive to Loose Park and kiss. They'd be parked in a dark spot near the rose garden, and joggers would pass within a few feet of the car. Ann May would hear the rhythmic padding footfalls, or she'd see a flash of reflector tape on the back of someone's sweatsuit.

At first she was stiff and scared, and she couldn't stop her brain from narrating what was happening inside the car: we're kissing now; he's touching my neck. But as the minutes passed, her feet went numb, her knees dissolved, and she sank into sensation, into pleasure.

They were beyond simple kisses now. His hand slid down into her pants, and she felt herself shifting; she was lifting her pelvis, trying to get closer to his fingers though it made no sense to do so—he was already touching her. They were already close. This is how girls get pregnant on prom night, thought Ann May. They go a little further and then a little more. If she and Jerry had been in a more private place, if they'd had more time than just the dinner break, Ann May might have let things keep going herself.

Once Jerry brought two glasses and some wine, which he drank while Ann May pretended to. "You should see what happens when people get drinking," he said. "At bars, you're talking to some woman, and she seems sort of so-so, sort of plain looking, then a few beers later, she's Miss Universe, she's Christie Brinkley. And you start looking better to her, too, and the next thing you know, you're in someone's apartment, mashing on the couch." He lifted his glass and took a sip. He looked at Ann May. "You're beautiful," he said.

On nights they went to the park, Ann May didn't eat until after ten. When she got home, she was ravenous. She would search the shelves in her parents' refrigerator and eat whatever she found there: mashed potatoes or cold pork and beans. She stood in the middle of her parents' kitchen holding a small plastic container, shoveling food into her mouth with her fingers.

She thought of the hairs that grew thick in his ears and the way he ran his tongue over his teeth. Who was he? she wondered. Just someone who didn't like to eat steakburgers alone? He sold copiers, had territories in St. Joe and Kansas City. Business was good, he said, but sometimes he felt lonely.

He lived nearby; he wasn't married. He was an amateur geologist who liked to poke around in rock shops. He loved quartz, but the best specimens were too expensive to buy.

One day he asked Ann May if she liked rocks.

"I guess so," she said, though the rocks she pictured were the ones the neighbor girls had pelted her with. Dusty gray gravel, driveway rocks. She thought of telling him the story, but before she had a chance, he was talking again, describing some strange formations he'd seen in Montana.

I'd like more," Jerry said one night. "I'd like to be intimate with you. Would you like that?"

"I guess so," said Ann May. She thought of the benefits Julie had promised—sex cleared the complexion, burned calories, improved circulation to the feet. She thought of the times in Jerry's car, her body urging her on.

"You don't want to be a virgin all your life," said Jerry. "Do you?"

Ann May shrugged. She wasn't sure how to answer. She'd already been a virgin all her life. It was all she'd ever been so far.

"Of course you don't," said Jerry. "Of course not."

It's natural," said Julie. "You're answering the call of the wild."

"I'm not a chimpanzee," Ann May protested. "I'm not a gorilla."

It was past ten, and the library was closed. Jerry was in the enclosed lobby, waiting to pick her up. Ann May could see him standing in front of the exhibit case, studying the display—ten or so books about butterflies, set against a backdrop of construction-paper grass. Julie grabbed Ann May's arm, held on to it. "Use a condom," she whispered. "I'm dead serious about this—even if he doesn't want to, you've got to insist. Promise me."

She stared steadily and held on to Ann May's arm until Ann May said, "I promise," and yanked herself free.

"Have fun," said Julie. "Get wild."

Jerry's apartment was clean but bare. Sofa, coffee table, stereo, TV, stove, refrigerator, dresser, bed. Ann May could almost understand why he preferred spending time in the car. At least he had a few decorations there: a pine-tree air freshener dangling from the windshield, a Chiquita banana sticker on the dashboard. The only decorations in the apartment were the miniblinds on the windows. Ann May drank a glass of water and ate a few Triscuits from the box Jerry offered. From the stereo came soft music that Ann May did not recognize. Removing his shoes, Jerry swung his feet up on the coffee table. "Go ahead," he said. "You, too, Ann May. Get comfortable."

"In a minute." She held up her glass. "When I finish my water." She thought of the romance novels she'd read. In the books, seduction scenes took place in luxurious rooms; there were roaring fireplaces and red velvet draperies and zebra rugs. Of course, she hadn't expected Jerry to own a castle or even a house, but in this plain apartment, drinking lukewarm tap water and nibbling stale crackers, she had trouble feeling romantic. She was nervous; she wasn't sure why she'd agreed to come here. And she was cold; the thin green silk blouse was not enough to keep her warm, but he'd asked her to wear it.

Jerry touched her shoulder, then rubbed the collar of the blouse between two fingers. "I just think it's amazing, don't you, that little worms made this shirt—the silk, I mean."

Ann May nodded. She took a sip of water.

"Is it saliva?" he said. "Secretions? Think if we could take our spit and make things out of it. Scarves and things." He sat quietly for a minute, musing.

"Where are your rocks?" asked Ann May. "Where's your collection?"

"In boxes," said Jerry. "I'll show you sometime." He rubbed her shoulder vigorously, as if she'd asked him to scratch a mosquito bite for her. "I should have gotten some wine."

"Oh, well," she said. "I don't mind."

When Jerry moved his hand to the front of her blouse, Ann May stayed still. She kept her hands in her lap while he unfastened the buttons one by one. She watched as he carefully laid the blouse on the table.

Why didn't he just buy a silk shirt for himself? thought Ann May. Silk underwear, silk pajamas, silk slacks, silk socks—what did he need her for?

He stood over her, placed a hand heavily on each shoulder, kissed her. She felt his tongue in her mouth, soft, then harder, and she lost track of where her own tongue was. He undid the snap on her jeans and pulled at the zipper. She adjusted her position, so his hand would fit more easily. Jerry's voice was soft. "Why don't you take off your pants?"

Her heart was pounding. This is it, she thought, this is prom night. Half sitting, half lying, Ann May tried to wriggle out of her jeans, but her underwear got twisted in the process, and it seemed for a moment that she was stuck. When she finally got her pants down to her ankles, she realized she'd have to take off her shoes. She reached to untie the laces and felt the rough weave of the sofa fabric against her bare skin.

"Nice," said Jerry, stroking her shoulder softly, then moving his finger along her skin to her breast. "It's like vanilla, so white." She didn't tell Jerry that vanilla was brown when you bought it in the store, when you found it on a kitchen shelf. Vanilla was only white in ice cream. He held her nipple between his thumb and forefinger, and the nipple hardened as it would in cold weather or cold water.

When he kissed her again, his lips seemed loose; his mouth was too wet, too open. Turning her head away, Ann May focused on the wall behind the sofa. Though the surface had looked smooth from a distance, up close the wall was as pocked and bumpy as a teenager's pimpled face. Jerry was tickling her ear with his tongue, and without really thinking about what she was doing, Ann May put her hand up and brushed him away.

She had liked the kissing earlier—she ought to be feeling excited now. But instead she felt restless and exposed; she felt as if a stranger in a public restroom had flung open the door to her stall and found her sitting on the toilet.

It wasn't the testicle. It was the rest, the oily shine of his face and the things he said: Think if we could take our spit and make things out of it.

He touched his lips to her neck.

She knew she didn't love him. And yet—why not go along with it? Jerry was here; he was interested; he was available. She was sitting naked on his couch—she was this close. She had three lubricated condoms in her purse. Why be the only person left out of this secret?

Why not?

Ann May pulled away, and Jerry's hand dropped. "What's wrong?" he asked.

She shook her head. Julie was going to ask what happened. What was she going to tell Julie? *Nothing.* She'd smile shyly and hang her head, and Julie would sock her in the arm and whoop. If Julie asked, Ann May would say it was all right. "Kind of slippery," she'd say.

"Honey, what's wrong?"

"I'm not ready." Ann May stood up. She folded her arms in front of her chest, turned her back to him, moved away. She thought of the romance books she'd read—in those books, "I'm not ready" meant "Kiss me some more."

So what if she was a virgin for the rest of her life? What did she care? Penis or no, she enjoyed the smell of roses, the taste of ice cream, the little waves exchanged with the firemen as she walked home from work. She liked sneaking out of the house as the sun was coming up, and plodding slowly around Loose Park. She liked grinding the coffee beans in the morning.

"Take your time," said Jerry. "Just relax." He motioned with his hand that she should come to the couch, that she should sit, but Ann May stayed where she was. She stayed standing. Jerry smiled. "Did I ever tell you about the time I went to Winstead's and ordered a skyscraper soda all by myself?"

His voice became a distant droning—the soft, steady beat of a hummingbird's wings, the flap of a flag in the wind. His voice was white noise from the TV; it was the murmur of prayer from deep within a church. Ann May let herself slip into the hum. She stood before Jerry's mirror, swaying gently. Her hair hung down, spread across her body like moss, some fabulous, frizzy moss. Her breasts sagged, and she noted the little hairs that grew around the nipples. She'd never understood these sparse hairs—did they serve a purpose or were they simply ornamental? Dropping her gaze, she studied her legs—they looked the same as ever, but they felt stronger since she'd started running; they felt more substantial.

"No one could believe it," said Jerry. "I ate the whole thing."

Ann May thought of being married to Jerry. Suppose her parents had arranged her marriage, the way people used to do in India, suppose Jerry had been selected as her partner. Would the rest of her life consist of going to Winstead's and listening to him talk about the desserts he'd eaten there once upon a time?

She retrieved the green shirt from the table. She felt a little guilty taking it—his silky fantasy—but she had to wear something. At least that was all she was taking from him.

"Good night," said Ann May when she was buttoned and tucked and zipped.

Jerry's face was chalky, expressionless. "Maybe another night?" he asked.

"No," said Ann May. "I don't think so."

Jerry nodded. He didn't offer to drive her home, and Ann May didn't ask him to. She walked down the long, carpeted corridor, past eight other apartments, and down the stairs. Opening the front door, she stepped out onto the sidewalk. The Dumpster at the side of the building was piled high with empty cardboard boxes; bulging black garbage bags were stacked nearby.

She'd tell Julie the truth eventually, and Ann May could predict what would happen: Julie would look at her with pity. She'd pat Ann May's arm and try to comfort her.

Ann May would gently disengage herself from Julie's grip. She'd say, "Don't worry about it."

In the apartment building, lights shone from every window. One of those windows belonged to Jerry, and Ann May knew she could go back there. She could have him if she wanted him.

Standing on the sidewalk, she smiled. It was close to midnight, and the traffic on J. C. Nichols Parkway was light, single cars separated by gaps of two or three blocks. In the dark sky, Ann May could make out three pale stars, three stars twinkling weakly.

She walked a few steps and then she was running, slowly for the first block, then faster and faster. The night had turned chilly, and the air scraped her throat, her lungs. When she turned onto Main Street, the traffic lights were blinking yellow. She could see them at intervals in the blocks ahead, blinking, blinking, waving her on.